BUBBA HO-TEP

D1803248

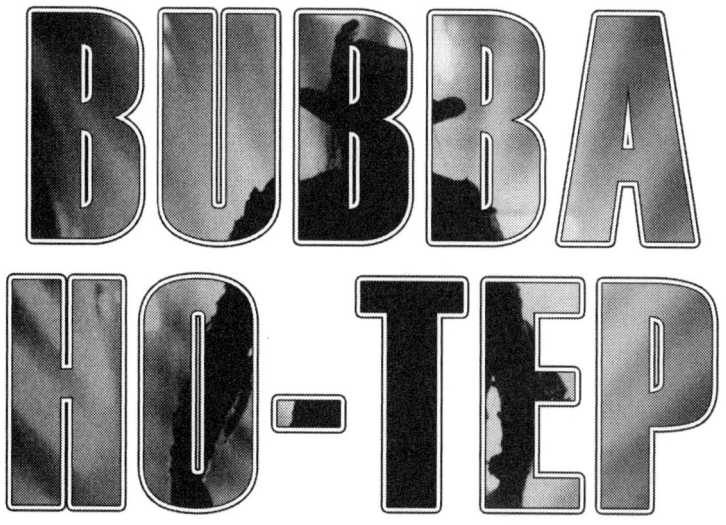

BUBBA HO-TEP

Story by
JOE R. LANSDALE

Screenplay by
DON COSCARELLI

NIGHT SHADE BOOKS
San Francisco & Portland

Bubba Ho-tep copyright © 1994 by Joe R. Lansdale
Bubba Ho-tep screenplay copyright © 2003 by Starway International, Inc.
Introductions copyright © 2003 by their respective authors
Cover & interior photographs copyright © 2003 by Starway International, Inc.
This edition of Bubba Ho-tep © 2005 by Night Shade Books
Interior design & layout by Garry Nurrish

All rights reserved. Printed in Canada.

This is a work of fiction. The characters and events portrayed in this book are ficticious, and any resemblance to real people or events is purely coincidental.

ISBN
1-59780-033-3

Night Shade Books
http://www.nightshadebooks.com

CONTENTS

Introduction to the Story — Joe R. Lansdale 1

The Story — Joe R. Lansdale 11

Introduction to the Screenplay — Don Coscarelli 49

The Screenplay — Don Coscarelli 57

BUBBA, UNCHAINED
or, How I Learned to Love a Story I Hated and How Don Coscarelli Made a Neat as Hell Film Out of It

by Joe R. Lansdale

My sister-in-law went to school with Elvis. You see, my brother, John, was sixteen, nearly seventeen when I was born. He moved to Memphis early on, tried to make it in the music business. Even recorded a record at Sun.

But, alas, it was not meant to be.

But he met Elvis.

Better, he met Mary, his wife to be, and, as I said, she had gone to school with Elvis.

My brother said the first time he met Elvis was in a theater (Lowes I think was the name, but don't quote me on that) where he showed John and Mary to their seats at a movie with a flashlight. Elvis was an usher. My brother said he thought then, Who is this guy? He has something? A star quality.

He was right.

The first music I ever remember hearing was Ernest Tubb and Elvis Presley. What people forget is, Elvis was once thought of as a country singer. An odd country singer, but a country singer nonetheless. In fact, he sang some country classics. Blue Moon Over Kentucky, a Bill Monroe favorite being an example.

Though, coming from Elvis, it sounded quite a bit different.

Soon, he was called the Hillbilly Cat, and the music he was singing was labeled rockabilly. It was a Southern creation. Later, as more and more performers contributed, it became known as rock and roll.

But, hell, you knew that.

I tell you this to explain why I have a strong connection to Elvis.

My brother and his wife.

The first music I remember.

And a haircut.

I got screwed on the haircut deal.

I was a kid, and my hair was getting kind of long, and I hated to go to the barber, and my mother, she says, if you'll go to the barber, we'll get it cut like Elvis's.

I thought, wow, Elvis. I'll get a haircut and come out with this cool wad of hair hanging down on my forehead.

She said, "We'll get you a crewcut. That's what Elvis has."

She didn't lie. He had just joined the army. And, after my trip to the barber, I had a crewcut too.

Not what I wanted. I cried.

Some years later I read a book about Elvis. I think it came out about the time he died straining at stool on the toilet. It told about the real Elvis. It was written by his body guards.

It had the ring of authenticity.

It was sad, really. It gave me and a fine writer named Lewis Shiner the idea to write an Elvis book. Our idea is that he didn't die, but went into hiding. This was before all the Elvis sightings. We did a proposal, sent it to our agent, who assured us there was no interest in Elvis stories, and so, the project was dead.

Not long after, there was a boom in all things Elvis.

Typical.

But, I still thought about Elvis.

He had been a boyhood hero. I still loved his music. The old and middle period stuff especially. I had seen all of his terrible movies. Even then I knew they sucked, but, man, he was so cool.

What happened?

Elvis had it all, and pissed it away. When he died, I wanted to cry like the time I got that crewcut, but this time, all I did was fell depressed for the old boy.

All that fame, and in the end, he was just some fucked up hillbilly on drugs. A talented hillbilly on drugs, but, shit man, it was like someone gave you a steak and you weren't happy until you shit on it.

Bless his rich ignorant heart.

We know a lot more about John Kennedy now, but once upon a time he was a knight in shining armor. Still one of our great presidents, but a lot more human than we knew then.

He gave us hope. He gave us the feeling that we could accomplish anything we wanted to do. He pushed education, reading, thinking. It was a big influence on us of the baby boom generation. We saw pictures of him and his family out playing football, and they were all so pretty and happy and healthy. He also pushed the idea of health, being physical. In other words, the Greek idea.

He was young.

He was vibrant (we didn't know about his health issues then, but that means nothing).

Good looking.

Had a beauty for a wife. And she had brains.

He seemed to have a happy marriage. (Remember, this was before we knew he was throwing the sausage to anything he could throw it to, and as often as he could throw it to them.)

He knew all the hip people.

Cool cat, that was John Kennedy.

And then one day in Dallas it was all over.

Camelot, as the White House was known during his brief tenure as president, was no more.

It was like the world had shifted on its axis with three snaps from Oswald's rifle (just for the record: yeah, I believe he did it alone).

An explosion of blood, a spinning away of skull fragments, and we entered into a dark time.

We've never quite come out of it.

Maybe it was always there, but for those of us called the Baby Boomers, that was our first real exposure to it.

Oh, we knew about the bomb. That hung over our heads like . . . well, a bomb. A big bomb. Atomic Bomb. A-Bomb we called it. A firecracker compared to what we have now. But we all thought one of those babies goes off, things get contaminated, next morning, next week, we're battling giant ants and lizards. And if all that happens, well, it's a good time for those aliens, guys in the flying saucers everyone was seeing, it was a good time for them to move in and take over. So yeah, we had that fear. Ours was the first generation under the shadow of the bomb, and the shadow was actually bigger then than the seventies, eighties or nineties. Though, the way things are going as of this writing in 2003, the shadow grows again . . . But, I'll not ramble. I will not.

Promise.

Stopping now.

I was talking about how the world seemed to shift.

John Kennedy was dead.

Boris Karloff. THE MUMMY. The first and best mummy movie of all time. I do like the new mummy films, but this one, man, it was creepy. And Karloff, he was never better. Never.

No real special effects.

Boris is only wrapped in the mummy rags at the first of the film, and briefly. Rest of the time he just looks like a dead body left out in the sun and the rain for a week or so.

I was a young kid. Saw it on television. Creeped the shit out of me. I saw all those old Universal films, and later the Hammer stuff. The mummy films led to my having an interest in ancient Egypt. That led to me majoring in archeology for the short time I went to college. I changed the major a few times, but for a time, anthropology and archeology were my interest. (Now that I think about it, don't know if I ever formally majored in archeology. Well, hell, if I didn't, I meant to.)

I still read archeology. I still read about mummies.

I like that stuff.

My mother taught me to read at a very early age.

My first book was Uncle Remus. Not politically correct now, but, frankly, great stories.

I then read comics. Comics were important to me. I loved the imagery.

The way all kinds of ideas, all kinds of genres, could be mixed at the drop of a hat.

Loved that stuff.

I owe a lot to my mother. She not only taught me to read, she encouraged me to read. She taught me respect for writers early on. Many years later, she had a terrible car accident. Her mind was lost for a time, and finally, when it did return, she was like a creature out of Invasion of The Body Snatchers. She looked like my Mom, but . . . she wasn't.

She had no emotion.

Eventually, she regained her emotions, but there were still weird spells. She was never the same.

Much to our dismay, my brother and I had to put her in a rest home in a small East Texas town. One of those towns that's got the coming and going sign on the same post.

It was close to my brother's house, an hour and a half away from me.

We could visit her a lot that way, her being close.

But the rest home. God, it depressed me. It was actually a pretty good one, but when I came to visit, I thought, how odd this feels. Poor Mom.

There were all sorts of little rest home intrigues. Sex was still considered, and, from time to time it happened. Men, they got in there, they didn't quit wanting to wet the pickle, they just had to work harder to make the pickle . . . well, pickle. Bathroom trips were a big deal. Hard for some to do. Everything was measured in urination and defecation. People talked to themselves, sang to themselves, carried on conversations with you as if you were their long lost son.

I thought, will I end up here too? Or rather one just like it? Talking to myself, thinking about the old days when I could get a boner, being proud if I did get one, wondering if I was going to shit myself if I didn't get my bed pan soon enough?

Not pleasant thoughts, gentle readers.

I never thought I'd have to put my mother in a place like that, but then I never realized that she would get to be more than just old. She was damaged, and would need twenty-four hour care.

I was beginning to make a little money as a writer then, and I was able to make her life a lot more comfortable than I might have a few years before, but she couldn't have in-home care. She was a total invalid. There was no choice. She had to go in the rest home.

It was great to take her out of that joint from time to time, and when I took her back, I always felt depressed. As if there was some kind of malignant spirit hanging over the place.

It creeped me.

Once upon a time I was asked to write a story for a book called ELVIS IS DEAD, or some such thing. The title changed a few times, so I'm not sure anymore what the title was and I'm too lazy to look. I sat down thinking, now, what in the hell do I have to say about Elvis?

I discovered that I really was pissed at how he had treated himself. How he had ended his life. He was a poor Southern boy like me, and he had risen to heights of fame that were beyond understanding. He had it made. He could have had anything he wanted and lived anyway he wanted, and he ended up living like trailer trash in a great mansion on a hill, mooning about the death of his mother, eating peanut butter and jelly sandwiches, fried no less, packing on pounds, freezing up his colon, swelling up his heart, looking at people fuck through a mirrored wall, taping it for his entertainment. Or so the book ELVIS, WHAT HAPPENED said. The one written by the bodyguards.

Shit, how the mighty had fallen.

So, I'm thinking, hey, maybe he would have turned around. Maybe if he had had a second chance.

I thought: Hey, what if all this Elvis impersonation stuff had another side. Like, there's this guy in the rest home who thinks he's Elvis. I could write about that. He might not be Elvis, but he could represent him.

Represent another chance for the King.

Then I thought, what if he is Elvis? What if, Elvis didn't die like we thought? Say he survived, and he's really got a second chance.

Now, that would be cool.

But, uh, in what way has he got a second chance?

And if he did survive, how did he?

Unlike mine and Lewis's idea that he had just gone into hiding, and everyone thought he was dead, I thought what if he switched out with an impersonator before, and it was really this other guy that died in his place. I thought, yeah, how about that? And, well, my mother was in that rest home, and that became the setting. And I got to thinking, might there not be other folks in this rest home who claim to be famous people? That would make it even harder for Elvis to be believed. Hell, he wasn't young anymore. Was anything like the charismatic legend he had once been, so, who would believe him?

Then I thought: well, who would some of these others believe themselves to be?

The Lone Ranger, or someone like him.

Dillenger. Yeah. That's good.

Hey, what about John Kennedy? He's an icon like Elvis.

And, hey, what if the guy who believes he's Kennedy is black?

And what about that air of misery that hangs over the rest home?

Wouldn't it be a great place to set a horror story? I mean, in many ways, it's pretty horrible as is, no supernatural agents need apply.

Say, I told myself, I could take the mummy and make him represent aging, fear of death, and I could even give it a comic twist. And, if I'm really cooking, maybe I can even manage to make it creepy.

Another thing. I really care about what happened to Elvis and Kennedy.

They were two of my childhood heroes. Things should have worked out better for them in the end.

Here's their chance.

So it all came together. A variety of sources. A variety of feelings.

I thought I had written the biggest Turkey in the history of writing.

The editor loved it.

The readers loved it.

It got nominated for an award.

People talked about it for years after. Even though it was rarely reprinted and has been seen and read by few. Still, it had a rep.

Don Coscarelli read it. He and I had wanted to work together for years.

But, Bubba Hotep?

I had never really learned to love the story. Perhaps because it was written during the time my mother was in the rest home. Perhaps because it was influenced by her being there. It also struck me as too loony to film.

I tried to talk Don out of it.

But no, Don was certain. And when Don is certain, you just got to move back and let him operate.

He optioned the story for several years.

I felt guilty taking his money.

He asked me to write the screenplay.

Passed on that. Didn't think it could be done properly.

He did a screenplay. I had a suggestion or two . . . too many narrators originally. He, of course, overruled me. (Still, later, he did drop the extra narrator, so maybe I'm not a total idiot.)

So now he had a script that read well, but still . . . filming Bubba Hotep?

Then, one day, he called and said he had raised the money and was going to film it.

I was shocked. He had done it. Better yet, he was able to get the guys we thought would be great in the roles. Bruce Campbell and Ossie Davis.

Wow. My son's favorite actor, the Bruce man. And one of my favorites, Ossie Davis.

Neat.

Still, I was skeptical.

My son and I flew out for a few days to watch the filming, and boy were we impressed. Bruce was amazing. And Ossie, well, at first I thought he was underplaying everything, and then, when I saw him on film, I realized he was the man. He knew exactly how much of this to give, how much of that to give.

The man is brilliant.

Anyway, it got filmed.

I saw it and loved it.

It's ninety five percent my story, and best of all, it didn't lose what mattered most to me about the story, which, I must admit, I've finally come to like.

It had real elderly heroes.

It gave them nobility.

The film makes you proud for them, happy. It really is a powerful and poignant piece of work.

And, oh yeah, it's got horror too.

I hope you enjoy rereading my story.

I hope you enjoy Don's script.

Our introductions.

Peace.

And, if you should find yourself in a rest home, watch your asshole, will you?

Joe R. Lansdale

BUBBA HO-TEP

by Joe R. Lansdale

Elvis dreamed he had his dick out, checking to see if the bump on the head of it had filled with pus again. If it had, he was going to name the bump Priscilla, after his ex-wife, and bust it by jacking off. Or he liked to think that's what he'd do. Dreams let you think like that. The truth was, he hadn't had a hard-on in years.

That bitch, Priscilla. Gets a new hairdo and she's gone, just because she caught him fucking a big tittied gospel singer. It wasn't like the singer had mattered. Priscilla ought to have understood that, so what was with her making a big deal out of it?

Was it because she couldn't hit a high note the same and as good as the singer when she came?

When had that happened anyway, Priscilla leaving?

Yesterday? Last year? Ten years ago?

Oh God, it came to him instantly as he slipped out of sleep like a soft turd squeezed free of a loose asshole for he could hardly think of himself or life in any context other than sewage, since so often he was too tired to do anything other than let it all fly in his sleep, wake up in an ocean of piss or shit, waiting for the nurses or the aides to come in and wipe his ass. But now it came to him. Suddenly he realized it had been years ago that he had supposedly died, and longer years than that since Priscilla left, and how old was she anyway? Sixty-five? Seventy?

And how old was he?

Christ! He was almost convinced he was too old to be alive, and had to be dead, but he wasn't convinced enough, unfortunately. He knew where he was now, and in that moment of realization, he sincerely wished he was dead. This was worse than death.

From across the room, his roommate, Bull Thomas, bellowed and coughed and moaned and fell back into painful sleep, the cancer gnawing at his insides like a rat plugged up inside a watermelon.

Bull's bellow of pain and anger and indignation at growing old and diseased was the only thing bullish about him now, though Elvis had seen photographs of him when he was younger, and Bull had been very bullish indeed. Thick-chested, slab-faced and tall. Probably thought he'd live forever, and happily. A boozing, pill-popping, swinging dick until the end of time.

Now Bull was shrunk down, was little more than a wrinkled sheet-white husk that throbbed with occasional pulses of blood while the carcinoma fed.

Elvis took hold of the bed's lift button, eased himself upright. He glanced at Bull. Bull was breathing heavily and his bony knees rose up and down like he was peddling a bicycle; his kneecaps punched feebly at the sheet, making puptents that rose up and collapsed, rose up and collapsed.

Elvis looked down at the sheet stretched over his own bony knees. He thought: *My God, how long have I been here? Am I really awake now, or am I dreaming I'm awake? How could my plans have gone so wrong? When are they going to serve lunch, and considering what they serve, why do I care? And if Priscilla discovered I was alive, would she come see me, would she want to see me, and would we still want to fuck, or would we have to merely talk about it? Is there finally, and really, anything to life other than food and shit and sex?*

Elvis pushed the sheet down to do what he had done in the dream. He pulled up his gown, leaned forward, and examined his dick. It was wrinkled and small. It didn't look like something that had dive-bombed movie starlet pussies or filled their mouths like a big zucchini or pumped forth a load of sperm frothy as cake icing. The healthiest thing about his pecker was the big red bump with the black ring around it and the pus-filled white center. Fact was, that bump kept growing, he was going to have to pull a chair up beside his bed and put a pillow in it so the bump would have some place to sleep at night. There was more pus in that damn bump than there was cum in his loins. Yep. The old diddlebopper was no longer a flesh cannon loaded for bare ass. It was a peanut too small to harvest; wasting away on the vine. His nuts were a couple of darkening, about-to-rot-grapes, too limp to produce juice for life's wine. His legs were stick and paper things with over-large, vein-swollen feet on the ends. His belly was such a bloat, it was a pain for him to lean forward and scrutinize his dick and balls.

Pulling his gown down and the sheet back over himself, Elvis leaned back and wished he had a peanut butter and banana sandwich fried in butter. There had been a time when he and his crew would board his private jet and fly clean across country just to have a special made fried peanut butter and 'nanner sandwich. He could still taste the damn things.

Elvis closed his eyes and thought he would awake from a bad dream, but didn't. He opened his eyes again, slowly, and saw that he was still where he had been, and things were no better. He reached over and opened his dresser drawer and got out a little round mirror and looked at himself.

He was horrified. His hair was white as salt and had receded dramatically. He had wrinkles deep enough to conceal outstretched earth worms, the big ones, the night crawlers. His pouty mouth no longer appeared pouty. It looked like the droopping waddles of a bulldog, seeming more that way because he was slobbering a mite. He dragged his tired tongue across his lips to daub the slobber, revealed to himself in the mirror that he was missing a lot of teeth.

Goddamn it! How had he gone from King of Rock and Roll to this? Old guy in a rest home in East Texas with a growth on his dick?

And what was that growth? Cancer? No one was talking. No one seemed to know. Perhaps the bump was a manifestation of the mistakes of his life, so many of them made with his dick.

He considered on that. Did he ask himself this question every day, or just now and then? Time sort of ran together when the last moment and the immediate moment and the moment forthcoming were all alike.

Shit, when was lunch time? Had he slept through it?

Was it about time for his main nurse again? The good looking one with the smooth chocolate skin and tits like grapefruits. The one who came in and sponge bathed him and held his pitiful little pecker in her gloved hands and put salve on his canker with all the enthusiasm of a mechanic oiling a defective part?

He hoped not. That was the worst of it. A doll like that handling him without warmth or emotion. Twenty years ago, just twenty, he could have made with the curled lip smile and had her eating out of his asshole. Where had his youth gone? Why hadn't fame denied old age and death, and why had he left his fame in the first place, and did he want it back, and could he have it back, and if he could, would it make any difference?

And finally, when he was evacuated from the bowels of life into the toilet bowl of the beyond and was flushed, would the great sewer pipe flow him to the other side where God would—in the guise of a great all-seeing turd with corn kernel eyes—be waiting with open turd arms, and would there be amongst the sewage his mother (bless her fat little heart) and father and friends, waiting with fried peanut butter and 'nanner sandwiches and ice cream cones, predigested, or course?

He was reflecting on this, pondering the afterlife, when Bull gave out with a hell of a scream, pooched his eyes damn near out of his head, arched his back, grease-farted like a blast from Gabriel's trumpet, and checked his tired old soul out of the Mud Creek Shady Grove Convalescence Home; flushed it on out and across the great shitty beyond.

Later that day, Elvis lay sleeping, his lips fluttering the bad taste of lunch—steamed zucchini and boiled peas—out of his belly. He awoke to a noise, rolled over to see a young attractive woman cleaning out Bull's dresser drawer. The curtains over the window next to Bull's bed were pulled wide open, and the sunlight was cutting through it and showing her to great advantage. She was blonde and Nordic-featured and her long hair was tied back with a big red bow and she wore big, gold, hoop earrings that shimmered in the sunlight. She was dressed in a white blouse and a short black skirt and dark hose and high heels. The heels made her ass ride up beneath her skirt like soft bald baby heads under a thin blanket.

She had a big, yellow, plastic trashcan and she had one of Bull's dresser drawers pulled out, and she was picking through it, like a magpie looking for bright things. She found a few coins, a pocket knife, a cheap watch. These were plucked free and laid on the dresser top, then the remaining contents of the drawer—Bull's photographs of himself when young, a rotten pack of rubbers (wishful thinking never deserted Bull), a bronze star and a purple heart from his performance in the Vietnam War—were dumped into the trashcan with a bang and a flutter.

Elvis got hold of his bed lift button and raised himself for a better look. The woman had her back to him now, and didn't notice. She was replacing the dresser drawer and pulling out another. It was full of clothes. She took out the few shirts and pants and socks and underwear, and laid them on Bull's bed remade now, and minus Bull, who had been toted off to be taxidermied, embalmed, burned up, whatever.

"You're gonna toss that stuff," Elvis said. "Could I have one of them pictures of Bull? Maybe that purple heart? He was proud of it."

The young woman turned and looked at him, "I suppose," she said. She went to the trashcan and bent over it and showed her black panties to Elvis as she rummaged. He knew the revealing of her panties was neither intentional or unintentional. She just didn't give a damn. She saw him as so physically and sexually non-threatening, she didn't mind if he got a birds-eye view of her; it was the same to her as a house cat sneaking a peek.

Elvis observed the thin panties straining and slipping into the caverns of her ass cheeks and felt his pecker flutter once, like a bird having a heart attack, then it laid down and remained limp and still.

Well, these days, even a flutter was kind of reassuring.

The woman surfaced from the trashcan with a photo and the purple heart, went over to Elvis's bed and handed them to him.

Elvis dangled the ribbon that held the purple heart between his fingers, said, "Bull your kin?"

"My daddy," she said.

"I haven't seen you here before."

"Only been here once before," she said. "When I checked him in."

"Oh," Elvis said. "That was three years ago, wasn't it?"

"Yeah. Were you and him friends?"

Elvis considered the question. He didn't know the real answer. All he knew was Bull listened to him when he said he was Elvis Presley and seemed to believe him. If he didn't believe him, he at least had the courtesy not to patronize. Bull always called him Elvis, and before Bull grew too ill, he always played cards and checkers with him.

"Just roommates," Elvis said. "He didn't feel good enough to say much. I just sort of hated to see what was left of him go away so easy. He was an all right guy. He mentioned you a lot. You're Callie, right?"

"Yeah," she said. "Well, he was all right."

"Not enough you came and saw him though."

"Don't try to put some guilt trip on me, Mister. I did what I could. Hadn't been for Medicaid, Medicare, whatever that stuff was, he'd have been in a ditch somewhere. I didn't have the money to take care of him."

Elvis thought of his own daughter, lost long ago to him. If she knew he lived, would she come to see him? Would she care? He feared knowing the answer.

"You could have come and seen him," Elvis said.

"I was busy. Mind your own business. Hear?"

The chocolate skin nurse with the grapefruit tits came in. Her white uniform crackled like cards being shuffled. Her little white nurse hat was tilted on her head in a way that said she loved mankind and made good money and was getting regular dick. She smiled at Callie and then at Elvis. "How are you this morning, Mr. Haff?"

"All right," Elvis said. "But I prefer Mr. Presley. Or Elvis. I keep telling you that. I don't go by Sebastian Haff anymore. I don't try to hide anymore."

"Why, of course," said the pretty nurse. "I knew that. I forgot. Good morning, Elvis."

Her voice dripped with sorghum syrup. Elvis wanted to hit her with his bed pan.

The nurse said to Callie: "Did you know we have a celebrity here, Miss Jones? Elvis Presley. You know, the rock and roll singer?"

"I've heard of him," Callie said. "I thought he was dead."

Callie went back to the dresser and squatted and set to work on the bottom drawer. The nurse looked at Elvis and smiled again, only she spoke to Callie. "Well, actually, Elvis is dead, and Mr. Haff knows that, don't you, Mr. Haff?"

"Hell no," said Elvis. "I'm right here. I ain't dead, yet."

"Now, Mr. Haff, I don't mind calling you Elvis, but you're a little confused, or like to play sometimes. You were an Elvis impersonator. Remember? You fell off a stage and broke your hip. What was it . . . Twenty years ago? It got infected and you went into a coma for a few years. You came out with a few problems."

"I was impersonating myself," Elvis said. "I couldn't do nothing else. I haven't got any problems. You're trying to say my brain is messed up, aren't you?"

Callie quit cleaning out the bottom drawer of the dresser. She was interested now, and though it was no use, Elvis couldn't help but try and explain who he was, just one more time. The explaining had become a habit, like wanting to smoke a cigar long after the enjoyment of it was gone.

"I got tired of it all," he said. "I got on drugs, you know. I wanted out. Fella named Sebastian Haff, an Elvis imitator, the best of them. He took my place. He had a bad heart and he liked drugs, too. It was him died, not me. I took his place."

"Why would you want to leave all that fame," Callie said, "all that money?" and she looked at the nurse, like *Let's humor the old fart for a lark.*

"Cause it got old. Woman I loved, Priscilla, she was gone. Rest of the women . . . were just women. The music wasn't mine anymore. I wasn't even me anymore. I was this thing they made up. Friends were sucking me dry. I got away and liked it, left all the money with Sebastian, except for enough to sustain me if things got bad. We had a deal, me and Sebastian. When I wanted to come back, he'd let me. It was all written up in a contract in case he wanted to give me a hard time, got to liking my life too good. Thing was, copy of the contract I had got lost in a trailer fire. I was living simple. Way Haff had been. Going from town to town doing the Elvis act. Only I felt like I was really me again. Can you dig that?"

"We're digging it, Mr. Haff . . . Mr. Presley," said the pretty nurse.

"I was singing the old way. Doing some new songs. Stuff I wrote. I was getting attention on a small but good scale. Women throwing themselves at me, cause they could imagine I was Elvis—only I was Elvis, playing Sebastian Haff playing Elvis . . . It was all pretty good. I didn't mind the contract being burned up. I didn't even try to go back and convince anybody. Then I had the accident. Like I was saying, I'd laid up a little money in case of illness, stuff like that. That's what's paying for here. These nice facilities. Ha!"

"Now, Elvis," the nurse said. "Don't carry it too far. You may just get way out there and not come back."

"Oh fuck you," Elvis said.

The nurse giggled.

Shit, Elvis thought. *Get old, you can't even cuss somebody and have it bother them. Everything you do is either worthless or sadly amusing.*

"You know, Elvis," said the pretty nurse, "we have a Mr. Dillinger here too. And a President Kennedy. He says the bullet only wounded him and his brain is in a fruit jar at the White House, hooked up to some wires and a battery, and as long as the battery works, he can walk around without it. His brain, that is. You know, he says everyone was in on trying to assassinate him. Even Elvis Presley."

"You're an asshole," Elvis said.

"I'm not trying to hurt your feelings, Mr. Haff," the nurse said. "I'm merely trying to give you a reality check."

"You can shove that reality check right up your pretty black ass," Elvis said.

The nurse made a sad little snicking sound. "Mr. Haff, Mr. Haff. Such language."

"What happened to get you here?" said Callie. "Say you fell off a stage?"

"I was gyrating," Elvis said. "Doing *Blue Moon,* but my hip went out. I'd been having trouble with it." Which was quite true. He'd sprained it making love to a blue haired old lady with ELVIS tattooed on her fat ass. He couldn't help himself from wanting to fuck her. She looked like his mother, Gladys.

"You swiveled right off the stage?" Callie said. "Now that's sexy."

Elvis looked at her. She was smiling. This was great fun for her, listening to some nut tell a tale. She hadn't had this much fun since she put her old man in the rest home.

"Oh, leave me the hell alone," Elvis said.

The women smiled at one another, passing a private joke. Callie said to the nurse: "I've got what I want." She scraped the bright things off the top of Bull's dresser into her purse. "The clothes can go to Goodwill or the Salvation Army."

The pretty nurse nodded to Callie. "Very well. And I'm very sorry about your father. He was a nice man."

"Yeah," said Callie, and she started out of there. She paused at the foot of Elvis's bed. "Nice to meet you, Mr. Presley."

"Get the hell out," Elvis said.

"Now, now," said the pretty nurse, patting his foot through the covers, as if it were a little cantankerous dog. "I'll be back later to do that . . . little thing that has to be done. You know?"

"I know," Elvis said, not liking the words "little thing."

Callie and the nurse started away then, punishing him with the clean lines of their faces and the sheen of their hair, the jiggle of their asses and tits. When they were out of sight, Elvis heard them laugh about something in the hall, then they were gone, and Elvis felt as if he were on the far side of Pluto without a jacket. He picked up the ribbon with the purple heart and looked at it.

Poor Bull. In the end, did anything really matter?

Meanwhile . . .

The Earth swirled around the sun like a spinning turd in the toilet bowl (to keep up with Elvis's metaphors) and the good old abused Earth clicked about on its axis and the hole in the ozone spread slightly wider, like a shy lady fingering open her vagina, and the South American trees that had stood for centuries, were visited by the dozer, the chainsaw and the match, and they rose up in burned black puffs that expanded and dissipated into minuscule wisps, and while the puffs of smoke dissolved, there were IRA bombings in London, and there was more war in the Mid-East. Blacks died in Africa of famine, the HIV virus infected a million more, the Dallas Cowboys lost again, and that Ole Blue Moon that Elvis and Patsy Cline sang so well about, swung around the Earth and came in close and rose over the Shady Grove Convalescent Home, shone its bittersweet, silver-blue rays down on the joint like a flashlight beam shining through a blue-haired lady's do, and inside the rest home, evil waddled about like a duck looking for a spot to squat, and Elvis rolled over in his sleep and awoke with the intense desire to pee.

All right, thought Elvis. *This time I make it.* No more piss or crap in the bed. (Famous last words.)

Elvis sat up and hung his feet over the side of the bed and the bed swung far to the left and around the ceiling and back, and then it wasn't moving at all. The dizziness passed.

Elvis looked at his walker and sighed, leaned forward, took hold of the grips and eased himself off the bed and clumped the rubber padded tips forward, and made for the toilet.

He was in the process of milking his bump-swollen weasel, when he heard something in the hallway—a kind of scrambling, like a big spider scuttling about in a box of gravel.

There was always some sound in the hallway, people coming and going, yelling in pain or confusion, but this time of night, three A.M., was normally quite dead.

It shouldn't have concerned him, but the truth of the matter was, now that he was up and had successfully pissed in the pot, he was no longer sleepy; he was still thinking about that bimbo, Callie, and the nurse (what the hell was her name?) with the tits like grapefruits, and all they had said.

Elvis stumped his walker backwards out of the bathroom, turned it, made his way forward into the hall. The hall was semi-dark, with every other light out, and the lights that were on were dimmed to a watery egg yoke yellow. The black and white tile floor looked like a great chessboard, waxed and buffed for the next game of life, and here he was, a semi-crippled pawn, ready to go.

Off in the far wing of the home, Old Lady McGee, better known in the home as The Blue Yodeler, broke into one of her famous yodels (she claimed to have sung with a Country and Western band in her youth) then ceased abruptly. Elvis swung the walker forward and moved on. He hadn't been out of his room in ages, and he hadn't been out of his bed much either. Tonight, he felt invigorated because he hadn't pissed his bed, and he'd heard the sound again, the spider in the box of gravel. (Big spider. Big box. Lots of gravel.) And following the sound gave him something to do.

Elvis rounded the corner, beads of sweat popping out on his forehead like heat blisters. Jesus. He wasn't invigorated now. Thinking about how invigorated he was had bushed him. Still, going back to his room to lie on his bed and wait for morning so he could wait for noon, then afternoon and night, didn't appeal to him.

He went by Jack McLaughlin's room, the fellow who was convinced he was John F. Kennedy, and that his brain was in the White House running on batteries. The door to Jack's room was open. Elvis peeked in as he moved by, knowing full well that Jack might not want to see him. Sometimes he accepted Elvis as the real Elvis, and when he did, he got scared, saying it was Elvis who had been behind the assassination.

Actually, Elvis hoped he felt that way tonight. It would at least be some acknowledgment that he was who he was, even if the acknowledgment was a fearful shriek from a nut.

'Course, Elvis thought, *maybe I'm nuts too. Maybe I am Sebastian Haff and I fell off the stage and broke more than my hip, cracked some part of my brain that lost my old self and made me think I'm Elvis.*

No. He couldn't believe that. That's the way they wanted him to think. They wanted him to believe he was nuts and he wasn't Elvis, just some sad old fart who had once lived out part of another man's life because he had none of his own.

He wouldn't accept that. He wasn't Sebastian Haff. He was Elvis Goddamn Aaron Fucking Presley with a boil on his dick.

'Course, he believed that, maybe he ought to believe Jack was John F. Kennedy, and Mums Delay, another patient here at Shady Grove, was Dillinger. Then again, maybe not. They were kind of scanty on evidence. He at least looked like Elvis gone old and sick. Jack was black—he claimed The Powers That Be had dyed him that color to keep him hidden—and Mums was a woman who claimed she'd had a sex change operation.

Jesus, was this a rest home or a nut house?

Jack's room was one of the special kind. He didn't have to share. He had money from somewhere. The room was packed with books and little luxuries. And though Jack could walk well, he even had a fancy electric wheelchair that he rode about in sometimes. Once, Elvis had seen him riding it around the outside circular drive, popping wheelies and spinning doughnuts.

When Elvis looked into Jack's room, he saw him lying on the floor. Jack's gown was pulled up around his neck, and his bony black ass appeared to be made of licorice in the dim light. Elvis figured Jack had been on his way to the shitter, or was coming back from it, and had collapsed. His heart, maybe.

"Jack," Elvis said.

Elvis clumped into the room, positioned his walker next to Jack, took a deep breath and stepped out of it, supporting himself with one side of it. He got down on his knees beside Jack, hoping he'd be able to get up again. God, but his knees and back hurt.

Jack was breathing hard. Elvis noted the scar at Jack's hairline, a long scar that made Jack's skin lighter there, almost grey. ("That's where they took the brain out," Jack always explained, "put it in that fucking jar. I got a little bag of sand up there now.")

Elvis touched the old man's shoulder. "Jack. Man, you okay?"

No response.

Elvis tried again. "Mr. Kennedy."

"Uh," said Jack (Mr. Kennedy).

"Hey, man. You're on the floor," Elvis said.

"No shit? Who are you?"

Elvis hesitated. This wasn't the time to get Jack worked up.

"Sebastian," he said. "Sebastian Haff."

Elvis took hold of Jack's shoulder and rolled him over. It was about as difficult as rolling a jelly roll. Jack lay on his back now. He strayed an eyeball at Elvis. He started to speak, hesitated. Elvis took hold of Jack's nightgown and managed to work it down around Jack's knees, trying to give the old fart some dignity.

Jack finally got his breath. "Did you see him go by in the hall? He scuttled like."

"Who?"

"Someone they sent."

"Who's they?"

"You know. Lyndon Johnson. Castro. They've sent someone to finish me. I think maybe it was Johnson himself. Real ugly. Real goddamn ugly."

"Johnson's dead," Elvis said.

"That won't stop him," Jack said.

Later that morning, sunlight shooting into Elvis's room through venetian blinds, Elvis put his hands behind his head and considered the night before while the pretty black nurse with the grapefruit tits salved his dick. He had reported Jack's fall and the aides had come to help Jack back in bed, and him back on his walker. He had clumped back to his room (after being scolded for being out there that time of night) feeling that an air of strangeness had blown into the rest home, an air that wasn't there the day before. It was at low ebb now, but certainly still present, humming in the background like some kind of generator ready to buzz up to a higher notch at a moment's notice.

And he was certain it wasn't just his imagination. The scuttling sound he'd heard last night, Jack had heard it, too. What was that all about? It wasn't the sound of a walker, or a crip dragging their foot, or a wheelchair creeping along, it was something else, and now that he thought about it, it wasn't exactly spider legs in gravel, more like a roll of barbed wire tumbling across tile.

Elvis was so wrapped up in these considerations, he lost awareness of the nurse until she said, "Mr. Haff!"

"What . . . ?" He saw that she was smiling and looking down at her hands. He looked too. There, nestled in one of her gloved palms was a massive, blue-veined hooter with a pus-filled bump on it the size of a pecan. It was *his* hooter and *his* pus-filled bump.

"You ole rascal," she said, and gently lowered his dick between his legs. "I think you better take a cold shower, Mr. Haff."

Elvis was amazed. That was the first time in years he'd had a boner like that. What gave here?

Then he realized what gave. He wasn't thinking about not being able to do it. He was thinking about something that interested him, and now, with something clicking around inside his head besides old memories and confusions, concerns about his next meal and going to the crapper, he had been given a dose of life again. He grinned his gums and what teeth were in them at the nurse.

"You get in there with me," he said, "and I'll take that shower."

"You silly thing," she said, and pulled his night gown down and stood and removed her plastic gloves and dropped them in the trash can beside his bed.

"Why don't you pull on it a little," Elvis said.

"You ought to be ashamed," the nurse said, but she smiled when she said it.

She left the room door open after she left. This concerned Elvis a little, but he felt his bed was at such an angle no one could look in, and if they did, tough luck. He wasn't going to look a gift hard-on in the pee-hole. He pulled the sheet over him and pushed his hands beneath the sheets and got his gown pulled up over his belly. He took hold of his snake and began to choke it with one hand, running his thumb over the pus-filled bump. With his other hand, he fondled his balls. He thought of Priscilla and the pretty black nurse and Bull's daughter and even the blue-haired fat lady with ELVIS tattooed on her butt, and he stroked harder and faster, and goddamn but he got stiffer and stiffer, and the bump on his cock gave up its load first, exploded hot pus down his thighs, and then his balls, which he thought forever empty, filled up with juice and electricity, and finally he threw the switch. The dam broke and the juice flew. He heard himself scream happily and felt hot wetness jetting down his legs, splattering as far as his big toes.

"Oh God," he said softly. "I like that. I like that."

He closed his eyes and slept. And for the first time in a long time, not fitfully.

Lunchtime. The Shady Grove lunch room.

Elvis sat with a plate of steamed carrots and broccoli and flaky roast beef in front of him. A dry roll, a pat of butter and a short glass of milk soldiered on the side. It was not inspiring.

Next to him, The Blue Yodeler was stuffing a carrot up her nose while she expounded on the sins of God, The Heavenly Father, for knocking up that nice Mary in her sleep, slipping up her ungreased poontang while she snored, and—bless her little heart—not even knowing it, or getting a clit throb from it, but waking up with a belly full of baby and no memory of action.

Elvis had heard it all before. It used to offend him, this talk of God as rapist, but he'd heard it so much now he didn't care. She rattled on.

Across the way, an old man who wore a black mask and sometimes a white stetson, known to residents and staff alike as Kemosabe, snapped one of his two capless cap pistols at the floor and called for an invisible Tonto to bend over so he could drive him home.

At the far end of the table, Dillinger was talking about how much whisky he used to drink, and how many cigars he used to smoke before he got his dick cut off at the stump and split so he could become a she and hide out as a woman. Now she said she no longer thought of banks and machine guns, women and fine cigars. She now thought about spots on dishes; the colors of curtains and drapes as coordinated with carpets and walls.

Even as the depression of his surroundings settled over him again, Elvis deliberated last night, and glanced down the length of the table at Jack (Mr. Kennedy) who headed its far end. He saw the old man was looking at him, as if they shared a secret. Elvis's ill mood dropped a notch; a real mystery was at work here, and come nightfall, he was going to investigate.

Swing the Shady Grove Convalescent Home's side of the Earth away from the sun again, and swing the moon in close and blue again. Blow some gauzy clouds across the nasty, black sky. Now ease on into three A.M.

Elvis awoke with a start and turned his head toward the intrusion. Jack stood next to the bed looking down at him. Jack was wearing a suit coat over his nightgown and he had on thick glasses. He said, "Sebastian. It's loose."

Elvis collected his thoughts, pasted them together into a not too scattered collage. "What's loose?"

"It," said Jack. "Listen."

Elvis listened. Out in the hall he heard the scuttling sound of the night before. Tonight, it reminded him of great locust wings beating frantically inside a small cardboard box, the tips of them scratching at the cardboard, cutting it, ripping it apart.

"Jesus Christ, what is it?" Elvis said.

"I thought it was Lyndon Johnson, but it isn't. I've come across new evidence that suggests another assassin."

"Assassin?"

Jack cocked an ear. The sound had gone away, moved distant, then ceased.

"It's got another target tonight," said Jack. "Come on. I want to show you something. I don't think it's safe if you go back to sleep."

"For Christ's sake," Elvis said. "Tell the administrators."

"The suits and the white starches," Jack said. "No thanks. I trusted them back when I was in Dallas, and look where that got my brain and me. I'm thinking with sand here, maybe picking up a few waves from my brain. Someday, who's to say they won't just disconnect the battery at the White House?"

"That's something to worry about, all right," Elvis said.

"Listen here," Jack said. "I know you're Elvis, and there were rumors, you know ... about how you hated me, but I've thought it over. You hated me, you could have finished me the other night. All I want from you is to look me in the eye and assure me you had nothing to do with that day in Dallas, and that you never knew Lee Harvey Oswald or Jack Ruby."

Elvis stared at him as sincerely as possible. "I had nothing to do with Dallas, and I knew neither Lee Harvey Oswald or Jack Ruby."

"Good," said Jack. "May I call you Elvis instead of Sebastian?"

"You may."

"Excellent. You wear glasses to read?"

"I wear glasses when I really want to see," Elvis said.

"Get 'em and come on."

Elvis swung his walker along easily, not feeling as if he needed it too much tonight. He was excited. Jack was a nut, and maybe he himself was nuts, but there was an adventure going on.

They came to the hall restroom. The one reserved for male visitors. "In here," Jack said.

"Now wait a minute," Elvis said. "You're not going to get me in there and try and play with my pecker, are you?"

Jack stared at him. "Man, I made love to Jackie and Marilyn and a ton of others, and you think I want to play with your nasty ole dick?"

"Good point," said Elvis.

They went into the restroom. It was large, with several stalls and urinals.

"Over here," said Jack. He went over to one of the stalls and pushed open the door and stood back by the commode to make room for Elvis's walker. Elvis eased inside and looked at what Jack was now pointing to.

Graffiti.

"That's it?" Elvis said. "We're investigating a scuttling in the hall, trying to discover who attacked you last night, and you bring me in here to show me stick pictures on the shit house wall?"

"Look close," Jack said.

Elvis leaned forward. His eyes weren't what they used to be, and his glasses probably needed to be upgraded, but he could see that instead of writing, the graffiti was a series of simple pictorials.

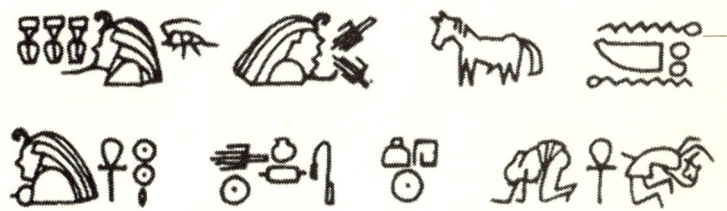

A thrill, like a shot of good booze, ran through Elvis. He had once been a fanatic reader of ancient and esoteric lore, like *The Egyptian Book of the Dead* and *The Complete Works of H.P. Lovecraft,* and straight away he recognized what he was staring at. "Egyptian hieroglyphics," he said.

"Right-a-reen-O," Jack said. "Hey, you're not as stupid as some folks made you out."

"Thanks," Elvis said.

Jack reached into his suit coat pocket and took out a folded piece of paper and unfolded it. He pressed it to the wall. Elvis saw that it was covered with the same sort of figures that were on the wall of the stall.

"I copied this down yesterday. I came in here to shit because they hadn't cleaned up my bathroom. I saw this on the wall, went back to my room and looked it up in my books and wrote it all down. The top line translates something like: *Pharaoh gobbles donkey goober.* And the bottom line is: *Cleopatra does the dirty.*"

"What?"

"Well, pretty much," Jack said.

Elvis was mystified. "All right," he said. "One of the nuts here, present company excluded, thinks he's Tutankhamun or something, and he writes on the wall in hieroglyphics. So what? I mean, what's the connection? Why are we hanging out in a toilet?"

"I don't know how they connect exactly," Jack said. "Not yet. But this . . . thing, it caught me asleep last night, and I came awake just in time to . . . well, he had me on the floor and had his mouth over my asshole."

"A shit eater?" Elvis said.

"I don't think so," Jack said. "He was after my soul. You can get that out of any of the major orifices in a person's body. I've read about it."

"Where?" Elvis asked. "*Hustler?*"

"*The Everyday Man or Woman's Book of the Soul* by David Webb. It has some pretty good movie reviews about stolen soul movies in the back, too."

"Oh, that sounds trustworthy," Elvis said.

They went back to Jack's room and sat on his bed and looked through his many books on astrology, the Kennedy assassination, and a number of esoteric tomes, including the philosophy book, *The Everyday Man or Woman's Book of the Soul.*

Elvis found that book fascinating in particular; it indicated that not only did humans have a soul, but that the soul could be stolen, and there was a section concerning vampires and ghouls and incubi and succubi, as well as related soul suckers. Bottom line was, one of those dudes was around, you had to watch your holes. Mouth hole. Nose hole. Asshole. If you were a woman, you needed to watch a different hole. Dick pee holes and ear holes—male or female—didn't matter. The soul didn't hang out there. They weren't considered major orifices for some reason.

In the back of the book was a list of items, related and not related to the book, that you could buy. Little plastic pyramids. Hats you could wear while channeling. Subliminal tapes that would help you learn Arabic. Postage was paid.

"Every kind of soul eater is in that book except politicians and science fiction fans," Jack said. "And I think that's what we got here in Shady Grove. A soul eater. Turn to the Egyptian section."

Elvis did. The chapter was prefaced by a movie still from *The Ten Commandments* with Yul Brynner playing Pharaoh. He was standing up in his chariot looking serious, which seemed a fair enough expression, considering the Red Sea, which had been parted by Moses, was about to come back together and drown him and his army.

Elvis read the article slowly while Jack heated water with his plug-in heater and made cups of instant coffee. "I get my niece to smuggle this stuff in," said Jack. "Or she claims to be my niece. She's a black woman. I never saw her before I was shot that day in Dallas and they took my brain out. She's part of the new identity they've given me. She's got a great ass."

"Damn," said Elvis. "What it says here, is that you can bury some dude, and if he gets the right tanna leaves and spells said over him and such bullshit, he can come back to life some thousands of years later, and to stay alive, he has to suck on the souls of the living, and that if the souls are small, his life force doesn't last long. Small. What's that mean?"

"Read on . . . No, never mind, I'll tell you." Jack handed Elvis his cup of coffee and sat down on the bed next to him. "Before I do, want a Ding-Dong? Not mine. The chocolate kind. Well, I guess mine is chocolate, now that I've been dyed."

"You got Ding-Dongs?" Elvis asked.

"Couple of Pay Days and Baby Ruth too," Jack said. "Which will it be? Let's get decadent."

Elvis licked his lips. "I'll have a Ding-Dong."

While Elvis savored the Ding-Dong, gumming it sloppily, sipping his coffee between bites, Jack, coffee cup balanced on his knee, a Baby Ruth in one mitt, expounded.

"Small souls means those without much fire for life," Jack said. "You know a place like that?"

"If souls were fires," Elvis said, "they couldn't burn much lower without being out than here. Only thing we got going in this joint is the pilot light."

"Exactamundo," Jack said. "What we got here in Shady Rest is an Egyptian soul sucker of some sort. A mummy hiding out, coming in here to feed on the sleeping. It's perfect, you see. The souls are little, and don't provide him with much. If this thing comes back two or three times in a row to wrap his lips around some elder's asshole, that elder is going to die pretty soon, and who's the wiser? Our mummy may not be getting much energy out of this, way he would with big souls, but the prey is easy. A mummy couldn't be too strong, really. Mostly just husk. But we're pretty much that way ourselves. We're not too far off being mummies."

"And with new people coming in all the time," Elvis said, "he can keep this up forever, this soul robbing."

"That's right. Because that's what we're brought here for. To get us out of the way until we die. And the ones don't die first of disease, or just plain old age, he gets."

Elvis considered all that. "That's why he doesn't bother the nurses and aides and administrators? He can go unsuspected."

"That, and they're not asleep. He has to get you when you're sleeping or unconscious."

"All right, but the thing throws me, Jack, is how does an ancient Egyptian end up in an East Texas rest home, and why is he writing on shit house walls?"

"He went to take a crap, got bored, and wrote on the wall. He probably wrote on pyramid walls, centuries ago."

"What would he crap?" Elvis said. "It's not like he'd eat, is it?"

"He eats souls," Jack said, "so I assume, he craps soul residue. And what that means to me is, you die by his mouth, you don't go to the otherside, or wherever souls go. He digests the souls 'til they don't exist anymore—"

"And you're just so much toilet water decoration," Elvis said.

"That's the way I've got it worked out," Jack said. "He's just like anyone else when he wants to take a dump. He likes a nice clean place with a flush. They didn't have that in his time, and I'm sure he finds it handy. The writing on the walls is just habit. Maybe, to him, Pharaoh and Cleopatra were just yesterday."

Elvis finished off the Ding-Dong and sipped his coffee. He felt a rush from the sugar and he loved it. He wanted to ask Jack for the Pay Day he had mentioned, but restrained himself. Sweets, fried foods, late nights and drugs had been the beginning of his original downhill spiral. He had to keep himself collected this time. He had to be ready to battle the Egyptian soul-sucking menace.

Soul-sucking menace?

God. He was really bored. It was time for him to go back to his room and to bed so he could shit on himself, get back to normal.

But Jesus and Ra, this was different from what had been going on up until now! It might all be bullshit, but considering what was going on in his life right now, it was absorbing bullshit. It might be worth playing the game to the hilt, even if he was playing it with a black guy who thought he was John F. Kennedy and believed an Egyptian mummy was stalking the corridors of Shady Grove Convalescent Home, writing graffiti on toilet stalls, sucking people's souls out through their assholes, digesting them, and crapping them down the visitor's toilet.

Suddenly, Elvis was pulled out of his considerations. There came from the hall the noise again. The sound that each time he heard it reminded him of something different. This time it was dried corn husks being rattled in a high wind. He felt goose bumps travel up his spine and the hairs on the back of his neck and arms stood up. He leaned forward and put his hands on his walker and pulled himself upright.

"Don't go in the hall," Jack said.

"I'm not asleep."

"That doesn't mean it won't hurt you."

"It my ass, there isn't any mummy from Egypt."

"Nice knowing you, Elvis."

Elvis inched the walker forward. He was halfway to the open door when he spied the figure in the hallway.

As the thing came even with the doorway, the hall lights went dim and sputtered. Twisting about the apparition, like pet crows, were flutters of shadows. The thing walked and stumbled, shuffled and flowed. Its legs moved like Elvis' own, meaning not too good, and yet, there was something about its locomotion that was impossible to identify. Stiff, but ghostly smooth. It was dressed in nasty looking jeans, a black shirt and a black cowboy hat that came down so low it covered where the thing's eyebrows should be. It wore large cowboy boots with the toes curled up, and there came from the thing a kind of mixed-stench: a compost pile of mud, rotting leaves, resin, spoiled fruit, dry dust and gassy sewage.

Elvis found that he couldn't scoot ahead another inch. He froze. The thing stopped and cautiously turned its head on its apple stem neck and looked at Elvis with empty eye sockets, revealing that it was, in fact, uglier than Lyndon Johnson.

Surprisingly, Elvis found he was surging forward as if on a zooming camera dolly, and that he was plunging into the thing's right eye socket, which swelled speedily to the dimensions of a vast canyon bottomed by blackness.

Down Elvis went, spinning and spinning, and out of the emptiness rushed resin-scented memories of pyramids and boats on a river, hot, blue skies, and a great silver bus lashed hard by black rain, a crumbling bridge and a charge of dusky water and a gleam of silver.

Then there was a darkness so caliginous it was beyond being called dark, and Elvis could feel and taste mud in his mouth and a sensation of claustrophobia beyond expression. And he could perceive the thing's hunger, a hunger that prodded him like hot pins, and then—

—there came a *popping* sound in rapid succession, and Elvis felt himself whirling even faster, spinning backwards out of that deep memory canyon of the dusty head, and now he stood once again within the framework of his walker, and the mummy—for Elvis no longer denied to himself that it was such—turned its head away and began to move again, to shuffle, to flow, to stumble, to glide, down the hall, its pet shadows screeching with rusty throats around its head. Pop! Pop! Pop!

As the thing moved on, Elvis compelled himself to lift his walker and advance into the hall. Jack slipped up beside him, and they saw the mummy in cowboy clothes traveling toward the exit door at the back of the home. When it came to the locked door, it leaned against where the door met the jam and twisted and writhed, squeezed through the invisible crack where the two connected. Its shadows pursued it, as if sucked through by a vacuum cleaner.

The popping sound went on, and Elvis turned his head in that direction, and there, in his mask, his double concho-studded holster belted around his waist, was Kemosabe, a silver Fanner Fifty in either hand. He was popping caps rapidly at where the mummy had departed, the black spotted red rolls flowing out from behind the hammers of his revolvers in smoky relay.

"Asshole!" Kemosabe said. "Asshole!"

And then Kemosabe quivered, dropped both hands, popped a cap from each gun toward the ground, stiffened, collapsed.

Elvis knew he was dead of a ruptured heart before he hit the black and white tile; gone down and out with both guns blazing, soul intact.

The hall lights trembled back to normal.

The administrators, the nurses and the aides came then. They rolled Kemosabe over and drove their palms against his chest, but he didn't breathe again. No more Hi-Yo-Silver. They sighed over him and clucked their tongues, and finally an aide reached over and lifted

Kemosabe's mask, pulled it off his head and dropped it on the floor, nonchalantly, and without respect, revealed his identity.

It was no one anyone really knew.

Once again, Elvis got scolded, and this time he got quizzed about what had happened to Kemosabe, and so did Jack, but neither told the truth. Who was going to believe a couple of nuts? Elvis and Jack Kennedy explaining that Kemosabe was gunning for a mummy in cowboy duds, a Bubba Ho-Tep with a flock of shadows roiling about his cowboy hatted head?

So, what they did was lie.

"He came snapping caps and then he fell," Elvis said, and Jack corroborated his story and when Kemosabe had been carried off, Elvis, with some difficulty, using his walker for support, got down on his knee and picked up the discarded mask and carried it away with him. He had wanted the guns, but an aide had taken those for her four-year-old son.

Later, he and Jack learned through the grapevine that Kemosabe's roommate, an 80-year-old man who had been in a semi-comatose condition for several years, had been found dead on the floor of his room. It was assumed Kemosabe had lost it and dragged him off his bed and onto the floor and the 80-year-old man had kicked the bucket during the fall. As for Kemosabe, they figured he had then gone nuts when he realized what he had done, and had wandered out in the hall firing, and had a heart attack.

Elvis knew different. The mummy had come and Kemosabe had tried to protect his roommate in the only way he knew how. But instead of silver bullets, his gun smoked sulphur. Elvis felt a rush of pride in the old fart.

He and Jack got together later, talked about what they had seen, and then there was nothing left to say.

Night went away and the sun came up, and Elvis, who had slept not a wink, came up with it and put on khaki pants and a khaki shirt and used his walker to go outside. It had been ages since he had been out, and it seemed strange out there, all that sunlight and the smells of flowers and the Texas sky so high and the clouds so white.

It was hard to believe he had spent so much time in his bed. Just the use of his legs with the walker these last few days had tightened the muscles, and he found he could get around better.

The pretty nurse with the grapefruit tits came outside and said: "Mr. Presley, you look so much stronger. But you shouldn't stay out too long. It's almost time for a nap and for us, to, you know . . . "

"Fuck off, you patronizing bitch," said Elvis. "I'm tired of your shit. I'll lube my own transmission. You treat me like a baby again, I'll wrap this goddamn walker around your head."

The pretty nurse stood stunned, then went away quietly.

Elvis inched his way with the walker around the great circular drive that surrounded the home. It was a half hour later when he reached the back of the home and the door through which the mummy had departed. It was still locked, and he stood and looked at it amazed. How in hell had the mummy done that, slipping through an indiscernible chink between door and frame?

Elvis looked down at the concrete that lay at the back of the door. No clues there. He used the walker to travel toward the growth of trees out back, a growth of pin-oaks and sweet gums and hickory nut trees that shouldered on either side of the large creek that flowed behind the home.

The ground tipped sharply there, and for a moment he hesitated, then reconsidered. *Well, what the fuck?* he thought.

He planted the walker and started going forward, the ground sloping ever more dramatically. By the time he reached the bank of the creek and came to a gap in the trees, he was exhausted. He had the urge to start yelling for help, but didn't want to belittle himself, not after his performance with the nurse. He knew that he had regained some of his former confidence. His cursing and abuse had not seemed cute to her that time. The words had bitten her, if only slightly. Truth was, he was going to miss her greasing his pecker.

He looked over the bank of the creek. It was quite a drop there. The creek itself was narrow, and on either side of it was a gravel-littered six feet of shore. To his left, where the creek ran beneath a bridge, he could see where a mass of weeds and mud had gathered over time, and he could see something shiny in their midst.

Elvis eased to the ground inside his walker and sat there and looked at the water churning along. A huge woodpecker laughed in a tree nearby and a jay yelled at a smaller bird to leave his territory.

Where had ole Bubba Ho-Tep gone? Where did he come from? How in hell did he get here?

He recalled what he had seen inside the mummy's mind. The silver bus, the rain, the shattered bridge, the wash of water and mud.

Well, now wait a minute, he thought. Here we have water and mud and a bridge, though it's not broken, and there's something shiny in the midst of all those leaves and limbs and collected debris. All these items were elements of what he had seen in Bubba Ho-Tep's head. Obviously there was a connection.

But what was it?

When he got his strength back, Elvis pulled himself up and got the walker turned, and worked his way back to the home. He was covered in sweat and stiff as wire by the time he reached his room and tugged himself into bed. The blister on his dick throbbed and he unfastened his pants and eased down his underwear. The blister had refilled with pus, and it looked nastier than usual.

It's a cancer, he determined. He made the conclusion in a certain final rush. They're keeping it from me because I'm old and to them it doesn't matter. They think age will kill me first, and they are probably right.

Well, fuck them. I know what it is, and if it isn't, it might as well be.

He got the salve and doctored the pus-filled lesion, and put the salve away, and pulled up his underwear and pants, and fastened his belt.

Elvis got his TV remote off the dresser and clicked it on while he waited for lunch. As he ran the channels, he hit upon an advertisement for Elvis Presley week. It startled him. It wasn't the first time it had happened, but at the moment it struck him hard. It showed clips from his movies, *Clambake, Roustabout,* several others. All shit movies. Here he was complaining about loss of pride and how life had treated him, and now he realized he'd never had any pride and much of how life had treated him had been quite good, and the bulk of the bad had been his own fault. He wished now he'd fired his manager, Colonel Parker, about the time he got into films. The old fart had been a fool, and he had been a bigger fool for following him. He wished too he had treated Priscilla right. He wished he could tell his daughter he loved her.

Always the questions. Never the answers. Always the hopes. Never the fulfillments.

Elvis clicked off the set and dropped the remote on the dresser just as Jack came into the room. He had a folder under his arm. He looked like he was ready for a briefing at the White House.

"I had the woman who calls herself my niece come get me," he said. "She took me downtown to the newspaper morgue. She's been helping me do some research."

"On what?" Elvis said.

"On our mummy."

"You know something about him?" Elvis asked.

"I know plenty."

Jack pulled a chair up next to the bed, and Elvis used the bed's lift button to raise his back and head so he could see what was in Jack's folder.

Jack opened the folder, took out some clippings, and laid them on the bed. Elvis looked at them as Jack talked.

"One of the lesser mummies, on loan from the Egyptian government, was being circulated across the United States. You know, museums, that kind of stuff. It wasn't a major exhibit, like the King Tut exhibit some years back, but it was of interest. The mummy was flown or carried by train from state to state. When it got to Texas, it was stolen.

"Evidence points to the fact that it was stolen at night by a couple of guys in a silver bus. There was a witness. Some guy walking his dog or something. Anyway, the thieves broke in the museum and stole it, hoping to get a ransom probably. But in came the worst storm in East Texas history. Tornadoes. Rain. Hail. You name it. Creeks and rivers overflowed. Mobile homes were washed away. Livestock drowned. Maybe you remember it . . . No matter. It was one hell of a flood.

"These guys got away, and nothing was ever heard from them. After you told me what you saw inside the mummy's head—the silver bus, the storm, the bridge, all that—I came up with a more interesting, and I believe, considerably more accurate scenario."

"Let me guess. The bus got washed away. I think I saw it today. Right out back in the creek. It must have washed up there years ago."

"That confirms it. The bridge you saw breaking, that's how the bus got in the water, which would have been as deep then as a raging river. The bus was carried downstream. It lodged somewhere nearby, and the mummy was imprisoned by debris, and recently it worked its way loose."

"But how did it come alive?" Elvis asked. "And how did I end up inside its memories?"

"The speculation is broader here, but from what I've read, sometimes mummies were buried without their names, a curse put on their sarcophagus, or coffin, if you will. My guess is our guy was one of those. While he was in the coffin, he was a drying corpse. But when the bus was washed off the road, the coffin was overturned, or broken open, and our boy was freed of coffin and curse. Or more likely, it rotted open in time, and the holding spell was broken. And think about him down there all that time, waiting for freedom, alive, but not alive. Hungry, and no way to feed. I said he was free of his curse, but that's not entirely true. He's free of his imprisonment, but he still needs souls.

"And now, he's free to have them, and he'll keep feeding unless he's finally destroyed... You know, I think there's a part of him, oddly enough, that wants to fit in. To be human again. He doesn't entirely know what he's become. He responds to some old desires and the new desires of his condition. That's why he's taken on the illusion of clothes, probably copying the dress of one of his victims.

"The souls give him strength. Increase his spectral powers. One of which was to hypnotize you, kinda, draw you inside his head. He couldn't steal your soul that way, you have to be unconscious to have that done to you, but he could weaken you, distract you."

"And those shadows around him?"

"His guardians. They warn him. They have some limited powers of their own. I've read about them in the *Every Man or Woman's Book of Souls*."

"What do we do?" Elvis asked.

"I think changing rest homes would be a good idea," Jack said. "I can't think of much else. I will say this. Our mummy is a nighttime kind of guy. Three A.M. actually. So, I'm going to sleep now, and again after lunch. Set my alarm for before dark so I can fix myself a couple cups of coffee. He comes tonight, I don't want him slapping his lips over my asshole again. I think he heard you coming down the hall about the time he got started on me the other night, and he ran. Not because he was scared, but because he didn't want anyone to find out he's around. Consider it. He has the proverbial bird's nest on the ground here."

After Jack left, Elvis decided he should follow Jack's lead and nap. Of course, at his age, he napped a lot anyway, and could fall asleep at any time, or toss restlessly for hours. There was no rhyme or reason to it.

He nestled his head into his pillow and tried to sleep, but sleep wouldn't come. Instead, he thought about things. Like, what did he really have left in life but this place? It wasn't much of a home, but it was all he had, and he'd be damned if he'd let a foreign, graffiti-writing, soul-sucking sonofabitch in an oversized hat and cowboy boots (with elf toes) take away his family member's souls and shit them down the visitors toilet.

In the movies he had always played heroic types. But when the stage lights went out, it was time for drugs and stupidity and the coveting of women. Now it was time to be a little of what he had always fantasized being.

A hero.

Elvis leaned over and got hold of his telephone and dialed Jack's room. "Mr. Kennedy," Elvis said when Jack answered. "Ask not what your rest home can do for you. Ask what you can do for your rest home."

"Hey, you're copping my best lines," Jack said.

"Well then, to paraphrase one of my own, 'Let's take care of business.'"

"What are you getting at?"

"You know what I'm getting at. We're gonna kill a mummy."

The sun, like a boil on the bright blue ass of day, rolled gradually forward and spread its legs wide to reveal the pubic thatch of night, a hairy darkness in which stars crawled like lice, and the moon crabbed slowly upward like an albino dog tick striving for the anal gulch.

During this slow rolling transition, Elvis and Jack discussed their plans, then they slept a little, ate their lunch of boiled cabbage and meat loaf, slept some more, ate a supper of white bread and asparagus and a helping of shit on a shingle without the shingle, slept again, awoke about the time the pubic thatch appeared and those starry lice began to crawl.

And even then, with night about them, they had to wait until midnight to do what they had to do.

Jack squinted through his glasses and examined his list. "Two bottles of rubbing alcohol?" Jack said.

"Check," said Elvis. "And we won't have to toss it. Look here." Elvis held up a paint sprayer. "I found this in the storage room."

"I thought they kept it locked," Jack said.

"They do. But I stole a hair pin from Dillinger and picked the lock."

"Great!" Jack said. "Matches?"

"Check. I also scrounged a cigarette lighter."

"Good. Uniforms?"

Elvis held up his white suit, slightly greyed in spots with a chili stain on the front. A white silk scarf, and the big gold and silver and ruby studded belt that went with the outfit lay on the bed. There were zippered boots from K-Mart. "Check."

Jack held up a grey business suit on a hanger. "I've got some nice shoes and a tie to go with it in my room."

"Check," Elvis said.

"Scissors?"

"Check."

"I've got my motorized wheelchair oiled and ready to roll," Jack said, "and I've looked up a few words of power in one of my magic books. I don't know if they'll stop a mummy, but they're supposed to ward off evil. I wrote them down on a piece of paper."

"We use what we got," Elvis said. "Well then. 2:45 out back of the place."

"Considering our rate of travel, better start moving about 2:30," Jack said.

"Jack," Elvis asked. "Do we know what we're doing?"

"No, but they say fire cleanses evil. Let's hope they, whoever they are, are right."

"Check on that, too," said Elvis. "Synchronize watches."

They did, and Elvis added: "Remember. The key words for tonight are *Caution* and *Flammable*. And *Watch Your Ass*."

The front door had an alarm system, but it was easily manipulated from the inside. Once Elvis had the wires cut with the scissors, they pushed the compression lever on the door, and Jack shoved his wheelchair outside, and held the door while Elvis worked his walker through. Elvis tossed the scissors into the shrubbery, and Jack jammed a paperback book between the doors to allow them re-entry, should re-entry be an option at a later date.

Elvis was wearing a large pair of glasses with multi-colored gem-studded chocolate frames and his stained white jump suit with scarf and belt and zippered boots. The suit was open at the front and hung loose on him, except at the belly. To make it even tighter there, Elvis had made up an Indian medicine bag of sorts, and stuffed it inside his jumpsuit. The bag contained Kemosabe's mask, Bull's purple heart, and the newspaper clipping where he had first read of his alleged death.

Jack had on his grey business suit with a black and red striped tie knotted carefully at the throat, sensible black shoes, and black nylon socks. The suit fit him well. He looked like a former president.

In the seat of the wheelchair was the paint-sprayer, filled with rubbing alcohol, and beside it, a cigarette lighter and a paper folder of matches. Jack handed Elvis the paint sprayer. A strap made of a strip of torn sheet had been added to the device. Elvis hung the sprayer over his shoulder, reached inside his belt and got out a flattened, half-smoked stogie he had been saving for a special occasion. An occasion he had begun to think would never arrive. He clenched the cigar between his teeth, picked the matches from the seat of the wheelchair, and lit his cigar. It tasted like a dog turd, but he puffed it anyway He tossed the folder of matches back on the chair and looked at Jack, said, "Let's do it, amigo."

Jack put the matches and the lighter in his suit pocket. He sat down in the wheelchair, kicked the foot stanchions into place and rested his feet on them. He leaned back slightly and flicked a switch on the arm rest. The electric motor hummed, the chair eased forward.

"Meet you there," said Jack. He rolled down the concrete ramp, on out to the circular drive, and disappeared around the edge of the building.

Elvis looked at his watch. It was nearly 2:45. He had to hump it. He clenched both hands on the walker and started truckin'.

Fifteen exhaustive minutes later, out back, Elvis settled in against the door, the place where Bubba Ho-Tep had been entering and exiting. The shadows fell over him like an umbrella. He propped the paint gun across the walker and used his scarf to wipe the sweat off his forehead.

In the old days, after a performance, he'd wipe his face with it and toss it to some woman in the crowd, watch as she creamed on herself. Panties and hotel keys would fly onto the stage at that point, bouquets of roses.

Tonight, he hoped Bubba Ho-Tep didn't use the scarf to wipe his ass after shitting him down the crapper.

Elvis looked where the circular concrete drive rose up slightly to the right, and there, seated in the wheelchair, very patient and still, was Jack. The moonlight spread over Jack and made him look like a concrete yard gnome.

Apprehension spread over Elvis like a dose of the measles. He thought: *Bubba Ho-Tep comes out of that creek bed, he's going to come out hungry and pissed, and when I try to stop him, he's going to jam this paint gun up my ass, then jam me and that wheelchair up Jack's ass.*

He puffed his cigar so fast it made him dizzy He looked out at the creek bank, and where the trees gaped wide, a figure rose up like a cloud of termites, scrabbled like a crab, flowed like water, chunked and chinked like a mass of oil field tools tumbling downhill.

Its eyeless sockets trapped the moonlight and held it momentarily before permitting it to pass through and out the back of its head in irregular gold beams. The figure that simultaneously gave the impression of shambling and gliding, appeared one moment as nothing more than a shadow surrounded by more active shadows, then it was a heap of twisted brown sticks and dried mud molded into the shape of a human being, and in another moment, it was a cowboy-hatted, booted thing taking each step as if it were its last.

Halfway to the rest home it spotted Elvis, standing in the dark framework of the door. Elvis felt his bowels go loose, but he was determined not to shit his only good stage suit. His knees clacked together like stalks of ribbon cane rattling in a high wind. The dog turd cigar fell from his lips.

He picked up the paint gun and made sure it was ready to spray. He pushed the butt of it into his hip and waited.

Bubba Ho-Tep didn't move. He had ceased to come forward. Elvis began to sweat more than before. His face and chest and balls were soaked. If Bubba Ho-Tep didn't come forward, their plan was fucked. They had to get him in range of the paint sprayer. The idea was he'd soak him with the alcohol, and Jack would come wheeling down from behind, flipping matches or the lighter at Bubba, catching him on fire.

Elvis said softly, "Come and get it, you dead piece of shit."

Jack had nodded off for a moment, but now he came awake. His flesh was tingling. It felt as if tiny ball bearings were being rolled beneath his skin. He looked up and saw Bubba Ho-Tep paused between the creek bank, himself, and Elvis at the door.

Jack took a deep breath. This was not the way they had planned it. The mummy was supposed to go for Elvis because he was blocking the door. But, no soap.

Jack got the matches and the cigarette lighter out of his coat pocket and put them between his legs on the seat of the chair. He put his hand on the gear box of the wheelchair, gunned it forward. He had to make things happen; had to get Bubba Ho-Tep to follow him, come within range of Elvis' spray gun.

Bubba Ho-Tep stuck out his arm and clotheslined Jack Kennedy. There was a sound like a rifle crack (no question Warren Commission, this blow was from the front), and over went the chair, and out went Jack, flipping and sliding across the driveway, the cement tearing his suit knees open, gnawing into his hide. The chair, minus its rider, tumbled over and came upright, and still rolling, veered downhill toward Elvis in the doorway, leaning on his walker, spray gun in hand.

The wheelchair hit Elvis' walker. Elvis bounced against the door, popped forward, grabbed the walker just in time, but dropped his spray gun.

He glanced up to see Bubba Ho-Tep leaning over the unconscious Jack. Bubba Ho-Tep's mouth went wide, and wider yet, and became a black toothless vacuum that throbbed pink as a raw wound in the moonlight; then Bubba Ho-Tep turned his head and the pink was not visible. Bubba Ho-Tep's mouth went down over Jack's face, and as Bubba Ho-Tep sucked, the shadows about it thrashed and gobbled like turkeys.

Elvis used the walker to allow him to bend down and get hold of the paint gun. When he came up with it, he tossed the walker aside, eased himself around, and into the wheelchair. He found the matches and the lighter there. Jack had done what he had done to distract Bubba Ho-Tep, to try and bring him down closer to the door. But he had failed. Yet by accident, he had provided Elvis with the instruments of mummy destruction, and now it was up to him to do what he and Jack had hoped to do together. Elvis put the matches inside his open chested outfit, pushed the lighter tight under his ass.

Elvis let his hand play over the wheelchair switches, as nimbly as he had once played with studio keyboards. He roared the wheelchair up the incline toward Bubba Ho-Tep, terrified, but determined, and as he rolled, in a voice cracking, but certainly reminiscent of him at his best, he began to sing "Don't Be Cruel," and within instants, he was on Bubba Ho-Tep and his busy shadows.

Bubba Ho-Tep looked up as Elvis roared into range, singing. Bubba Ho-Tep's open mouth irised to normal size, and teeth, formerly non-existent, rose up in his gums like little, black stumps. Electric locusts crackled and hopped in his empty sockets. He yelled something in Egyptian. Elvis saw the words jump out of Bubba Ho-Tep's mouth in visible hieroglyphics like dark beetles and sticks.[1]

Elvis bore down on Bubba Ho-Tep. When he was in range, he ceased singing, and gave the paint sprayer trigger a squeeze. Rubbing alcohol squirted from the sprayer and struck Bubba Ho-Tep in the face.

Elvis swerved, screeched around Bubba Ho-Tep in a sweeping circle, came back, the lighter in his hand. As he neared Bubba, the shadows swarming around the mummy's head separated and flew high up above him like startled bats.

The black hat Bubba wore wobbled and sprouted wings and flapped away from his head, becoming what it had always been, a living shadow. The shadows came down in a rush, screeching like harpies. They swarmed over Elvis' face, giving him the sensation of skinned animal pelts—blood-side in—being dragged over his flesh.

Bubba bent forward at the waist like a collapsed puppet, bopped his head against the cement drive. His black bat hat came down out

[1] *"By the unwinking red eye of Ra!"*

of the dark in a swoop, expanding rapidly and falling over Bubba's body, splattering it like spilled ink. Bubba blob-flowed rapidly under the wheels of Elvis' mount and rose up in a dark swell beneath the chair and through the spokes of the wheels and billowed over the front of the chair and loomed upwards, jabbing his ravaged, ever-changing face through the flittering shadows, poking it right at Elvis.

Elvis, through gaps in the shadows, saw a face like an old jack-o-lantern gone black and to rot, with jagged eyes, nose and mouth. And that mouth spread tunnel wide, and down that tunnel-mouth Elvis could see the dark and awful forever that was Bubba's lot, and Elvis clicked the lighter to flame, and the flame jumped, and the alcohol lit Bubba's face, and Bubba's head turned baby-eye blue, flowed jet-quick away, splashed upward like a black wave carrying a blazing oil slick. Then Bubba came down in a shuffle of blazing sticks and dark mud, a tar baby on fire, fleeing across the concrete drive toward the creek. The guardian shadows flapped after it, fearful of being abandoned.

Elvis wheeled over to Jack, leaned forward and whispered: "Mr. Kennedy."

Jack's eyelids fluttered. He could barely move his head, and something grated in his neck when he did. "The President is soon dead," he said, and his clenched fist throbbed and opened, and out fell a wad of paper. "You got to get him."

Jack's body went loose and his head rolled back on his damaged neck and the moon showed double in his eyes. Elvis swallowed and saluted Jack. "Mr. President," he said.

Well, at least he had kept Bubba Ho-Tep from taking Jack's soul. Elvis leaned forward, picked up the paper Jack had dropped. He read it aloud to himself in the moonlight: "You nasty thing from beyond the dead. No matter what you think and do, good things will never come to you. If evil is your black design, you can bet the goodness of the Light Ones will kick your bad behind."

That's it? thought Elvis. That's the chant against evil from the *Book of Souls?* Yeah, right, boss. And what kind of decoder ring does that come with? Shit, it doesn't even rhyme well.

Elvis looked up. Bubba Ho-Tep had fallen down in a blue blaze, but he was rising up again, preparing to go over the lip of the creek, down to wherever his sanctuary was.

Elvis pulled around Jack and gave the wheelchair full throttle. He gave out with a rebel cry. His white scarf fluttered in the wind as he thundered forward.

Bubba Ho-Tep's flames had gone out. He was on his feet. His head was hissing grey smoke into the crisp night air. He turned completely to face Elvis, stood defiant, raised an arm and shook a fist. He yelled, and once again Elvis saw the hieroglyphics leap out of his mouth. The characters danced in a row, briefly—

2

—and vanished.

Elvis let go of the protective paper. It was dog shit. What was needed here was action.

When Bubba Ho-Tep saw Elvis was coming, chair geared to high, holding the paint sprayer in one hand, he turned to bolt, but Elvis was on him.

Elvis stuck out a foot and hit Bubba Ho-Tep in the back, and his foot went right through Bubba. The mummy squirmed, spitted on Elvis' leg. Elvis fired the paint sprayer, as Bubba Ho-Tep, himself, and chair, went over the creek bank in a flash of moonlight and a tumble of shadows.

Elvis screamed as the hard ground and sharp stones snapped his body like a piñata. He made the trip with Bubba Ho-Tep still on his leg, and when he quit sliding, he ended up close to the creek.

Bubba Ho-Tep, as if made of rubber, twisted around on Elvis' leg, and looked at him.

Elvis still had the paint sprayer. He had clung to it as if it were a life preserver. He gave Bubba another dose. Bubba's right arm flopped way out and ran along the ground and found a hunk of wood that had washed up on the edge of the creek, gripped it, and swung the long arm back. The arm came around and hit Elvis on the side of the head with the wood.

2 *"Eat the dog dick of Anubis, you ass wipe!"*

Elvis fell backwards. The paint sprayer flew from his hands. Bubba Ho-Tep was leaning over him. He hit Elvis again with the wood. Elvis felt himself going out. He knew if he did, not only was he a dead sonofabitch, but so was his soul. He would be just so much crap; no after-life for him; no reincarnation; no angels with harps. Whatever lay beyond would not be known to him. It would all end right here for Elvis Presley. Nothing left but a quick flush.

Bubba Ho-Tep's mouth loomed over Elvis' face. It looked like an open manhole. Sewage fumes came out of it.

Elvis reached inside his open jumpsuit and got hold of the folder of matches. Laying back, pretending to nod out so as to bring Bubba Ho-Tep's ripe mouth closer, he thumbed back the flap on the matches, thumbed down one of the paper sticks, and pushed the sulphurous head of the match across the black strip.

Just as Elvis felt the cloying mouth of Bubba Ho-Tep falling down on his kisser like a Venus Flytrap, the entire folder of matches ignited in Elvis' hand, burned him and made him yell.

The alcohol on Bubba's body called the flames to it, and Bubba burst into a stalk of blue flame, singeing the hair off Elvis' head, scorching his eyebrows down to nubs, blinding him until he could see nothing more than a scalding white light.

Elvis realized that Bubba Ho-Tep was no longer on or over him, and the white light became a stained white light, then a grey light, and eventually, the world, like a Polaroid negative developing, came into view, greenish at first, then full of the night's colors.

Elvis rolled on his side and saw the moon floating in the water. He saw too a scarecrow floating in the water, the straw separating from it, the current carrying it away.

No, not a scarecrow. Bubba Ho-Tep. For all his dark magic and ability to shift, or to appear to shift, fire had done him in, or had it been the stupid words from Jack's book on souls? Or both?

It didn't matter. Elvis got up on one elbow and looked at the corpse. The water was dissolving it more rapidly and the current was carrying it away.

Elvis fell over on his back. He felt something inside him grate against something soft. He felt like a water balloon with a hole poked in it.

He was going down for the last count, and he knew it.

But I've still got my soul, he thought. Still mine. All mine. And the folks in Shady Grove, Dillinger, the Blue Yodeler, all of them, they have theirs, and they'll keep 'em.

Elvis stared up at the stars between the forked and twisted boughs of an oak. He could see a lot of those beautiful stars, and he realized now that the constellations looked a little like the outlines of great hieroglyphics. He turned away from where he was looking, and to his right, seeming to sit on the edge of the bank, were more stars, more hieroglyphics.

He rolled his head back to the figures above him, rolled to the right and looked at those. Put them together in his mind.

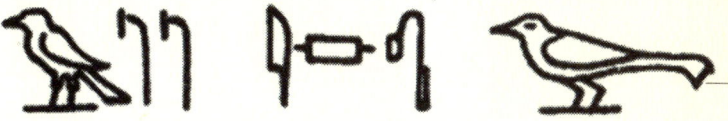

He smiled. Suddenly, he thought he could read hieroglyphics after all, and what they spelled out against the dark beautiful night was simple, and yet profound.

ALL IS WELL.

Elvis closed his eyes and did not open them again.

THE END

Thanks to

(Mark Nelson) for translating East Texas "Egyptian" Hieroglyphics.

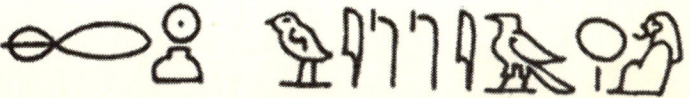

TO PUT DOWN A MUMMY
by Don Coscarelli

I am writing this introduction on the eve of the theatrical release of *Bubba Ho-tep* in the U.S. I have spent the past year traveling to film festivals across North America and around the world showing the film. I have been extremely gratified to find that the audience response has been fantastic and we have drawn turn-away crowds at every festival screening! I was fortunate enough to attend many of the festivals with both author Joe R. Lansdale and star Bruce Campbell, and even though the commercial fate of *Bubba Ho-tep* has not yet been written, we can sense that there is something special about this film.

It was in the summer of 1989 that I first heard of Joe R. Lansdale. I was visiting a local genre bookstore and asked an employee what was new in horror. He showed me a couple of books and then said, "You should try Joe Lansdale... he always has a high body count." That was all it took to make the sale and I went home that afternoon with a paperback copy of *The Drive In*. I had never read anything like Joe. His stuff was funny, scary, compelling, cinematic and all leavened with that amazing East Texas vernacular. I was amazed nobody had adapted one of his books into a film. Of course I loved *The Drive In* and tracked down Joe's phone number and called him up. I introduced myself and found Joe to be a helluva nice guy. Unfortunately, the rights to *The Drive In* were gone. But Joe recommended a couple of his other books and invited me to come visit him down in Nacogdoches, Texas. Over the next couple years I worked with Joe trying to get a couple of his other projects made into films with no luck. In late 1994 I spotted a new Lansdale short story collection on the bookshelves entitled *Writer of the Purple Rage*. While eagerly reading the dust jacket, I zeroed in on the log line of one of the stories. "Elvis battles Mummy" . . . hmmm, that sounds good!

I sat down and immediately read *Bubba Ho-tep*. What a story! It was crazy, ridiculous, funny as hell, scary and yet at the same time, tender and poignant. I have to admit that I actually shed a tear as Elvis saluted the dying JFK. I was convinced this would make a great movie.

People thought I was crazy. A movie about a 70-year-old Elvis, with cancer on his penis, fighting a soul-sucking Egyptian mummy in a rest home? Hell yeah!!! I immediately called up Joe and with the assistance of his agent Jimmy Vines we made a deal.

Now, how to adapt this 40 page short story into a 100 page screenplay?? The first question friends who read the story asked was, "You're not going to use the cancerous dick are you??" And at first, I tended to agree, thinking there was no way the MPAA ratings board would allow a subplot like that. But the more I thought about it, the more I realized it was an integral part of the story. So, like many decisions made during the process of creating a film, I just decided to leave it in until I was forced to remove it.

The other challenge the story posed was how to present an hour and a half movie about two old geezers in a decrepit old rest home. Could a modern, youthfully demographic audience tolerate such a tale? Without knowing who we would get to play our two heroes, this was a valid question. For quite a while I toyed with the idea of adding a few youthful characters, perhaps an orderly or janitor in his twenties, so there would be someone less than seven decades old reciting dialog. I ultimately decided that this would stray from the original intent of Joe's story and figured that, with the right actors, this risky endeavor just might work.

One of the great opportunities that the short story afforded was that it made very brief reference to what I saw as a potentially wonderful sequence, which was the concept of this character of Elvis switching places with impersonator Sebastian Haff. Many questions immediately popped into my mind . . . What would the first(and only) meeting be like between the King and this impersonator-who-

Director Don Coscarelli escorts the "King" (Bruce Campbell) to the set of "Bubba Ho-Tep".

would-be-King? What would this character of Elvis be thinking as he drove to this appointment with destiny in which he would renounce all the trappings of his former life and escape? What would it be like for the King, living a mundane life in a trailer park?

With the screenplay finished I received my first dose of harsh reality. No studio would seriously consider the *Bubba Ho-tep* screenplay, let alone fund it. They despised the elements that I believed made it great. Thankfully, the beauty of this story is in its simplicity (a great lesson for aspiring independent filmmakers). Except for a few key effects scenes . . . it's basically two guys talking in two or three rooms! Not expensive. So with the assistance of a couple familiar investors we cobbled together barely enough to make the film.

During this period, a very strange and bizarre act occurred which had a profound impact on the ultimate film of *Bubba Ho-tep*. One afternoon I came back to my office in Hollywood to find a message on the answering machine. A young man introduced himself as director Sam Raimi's assistant and proceeded to invite me to a special retrospective screening that Sam was hosting in Westwood of Spielberg's "Close Encounters of the Third Kind". I had met Sam several years previously when we were both working at Universal—he on *Darkman* and I on *Phantasm II*. He had been very supportive and had actually introduced me to the makeup-effects guys from *Evil Dead II*, who I hired for *Phantasm II* and who later went on to form the very highly regarded KNB Effects Group. I hadn't seen Sam in a few years, so the call came as a nice surprise. So I called him back to RSVP only to find out from his real assistant that there was no screening—the call had been a prank! Sam called back later and we had a good laugh about it. However, in the course of that conversation we traded stories about what we were working on and I told him about this mummy movie I was developing which featured "Elvis". Sam immediately seized on it. "You should talk to Bruce Campbell, he's a great actor." Before I could even comment, he said, "I'll have Bruce call you." Well, the rest is history. I was fortunate to meet Bruce and lucky to have him join the project and create a role which was described by *The Hollywood Reporter* critic David Hunter as "Bruce Campbell in a performance for the ages." And our un-credited collaborator, the crank caller, is still lurking out there somewhere . . . .

Bruce is a terrific actor who immersed himself in the role of "Elvis". Of course, with his make-up schedule, he had no choice. He was stuck in that old-age make-up for fourteen hours a day, and the way he dealt with it was to stay in character all day long. You'd hear him shuffling to the set in his PJ's and slippers greeting crew members with a wink and an "It's alright, mama." A modern-day Lon Chaney (*Man of a Thousand Faces*) the effects guys loved to work with Campbell because as they said, "Nobody plays make-up like Bruce." I also found his background as a director (*Hercules*, *Xena*) to be particularly helpful as Bruce was clever and quick with solutions when time was short.

From the outset there was only one person I ever considered for the role of President John F. Kennedy in *Bubba Ho-tep*, and that was the legendary Ossie Davis. Mr. Davis has a multi-faceted and storied career, having had great success not only as a stage and screen actor but also as a writer, historian and social activist. Ossie Davis has been starring in independent films since the 50's, including writing and directing what is considered to be one of the seminal "blaxpoitation" films, *Cotton Comes to Harlem*. He has had many starring roles on stage and Broadway, frequently co-starring with his wife, renowned actress Ruby Dee. In addition to winning such awards as the National Medal of Arts and the Screen Actors Guild Lifetime Achievement Award, Ossie has also been involved with a great many social causes. In 1965 he gave the eulogy at Malcolm X's funeral.

However, securing Ossie Davis for our film was a challenge. When I first approached Mr. Davis' agent, he read the screenplay and passed. He said that the screenplay had some okay moments between the characters but why did we need all that mummy business. Could we cut out the mummy? Of course not, I replied, and that was the end of the conversation. Over the next six months I did not relent. I kept calling, begging for him to give the screenplay to Ossie. I even asked my writer/director friend, Mick Garris, who had directed Ossie and Ruby in his epic mini-series, *The Stand*, to intercede and write a personal letter on my behalf to Ossie. Finally, one day there was a breakthrough. I called and the agent told me once again that he didn't like the screenplay, but that his client did. This was the break I had been seeking, and after some intense negotiations handled by our producer, Jason Savage, Ossie joined the cast!

The film shoot itself was challenging, to say the least, but we were extremely fortunate on several fronts. We found a rundown old hospital complex on the outskirts of LA that had been abandoned by the county. This saved us a lot of money as we had the run of the place and were able to shoot 98% of the film there. KNB Effects Group came on board and provided the outstanding old age makeup for the Elvis character at cost and one of their partners, Bob Kurtzman created the fantastic mummy prosthetic costume. Our costume designer, Shelley Kay, convinced the top Elvis jumpsuit fabricator in the nation, B+K Enterprises, to join our team and create the three authentic jumpsuits worn in the film by Bruce. In post production, two top visual effects designers (and major Bruce Campbell fans) David Hartman and Michael Smith enlisted at no pay (and brought along a team of artists from Sony) to create the amazing digital effects which included the hilarious visible hieroglyphics which tumble out of Bubba Ho-tep's mouth. We were also lucky to have D. Kerry Prior join up to design the scarab beetle sequence. Kerry created many of the dazzling killer sphere effects in several of the *Phantasm* films. On *Bubba Ho-tep* he was responsible for the design and fabrication of a dozen articulated insect models. We used only one digital effect in the sequence so, consequently, the vast majority were done the old fashioned way . . . with rubber. I can tell you it was one of the highlights of my career to have the honor of directing horror icon Bruce Campbell as he battled to the death with our prosthetic rubber insect props!

I would like to make special mention of the essential contribution made to our film by composer Brian Tyler. He added a depth and elegance to *Bubba Ho-tep* while creating a score that I think even the real Elvis would have liked. But in the end, it was the inspiration of Joe's great story that made our film what it is. Beneath all the humor, Bubba Ho-tep is essentially a story of friendship, courage in the face of death and ultimately, redemption.

As you read this you may understand how much effort has gone into the creation of our film. It has now taken several years to bring *Bubba Ho-tep* from story to screen. It would have been easy to poke fun at Elvis. Even though our character does and says many irreverent things in the film, I always believed that in the end it was crucial to treat him with the utmost respect. One critic said of *Bubba Ho-tep*,

"It's a loving tribute to the King." This was very gratifying and the kind of response I think that all of us were hoping for. All I can say is, "Thank you. Thank you very much."

After you have finished the book, I hope you will visit our website at www.bubbahotep.com and drop us an email. Bruce, Joe and I would love to hear your comments.

Don Coscarelli

BUBBA HO-TEP
The Screenplay
by Don Coscarelli

FADE IN:

Ho-tep (ho-tep') n.
1. Relative or descendent of the 17 Egyptian Dynasties, 3100—1500 B.C.
2. Family surname of an Egyptian pharaoh (king).

FADE OUT.

FADE IN:

Bubba (bub'uh) n.
1. Male from the Southern U.S.
2. Good ole boy
3. Cracker, red neck, trailer park resident.

FADE OUT.

FADE IN:

STOCK FOOTAGE
Grainy black and white GERMAN NEWSREEL FOOTAGE of an Egyptian archaeological dig. We see images of Egyptian laborers digging and scientists examining artifacts. A team of workers carry a desiccated mummy out of an underground tomb.

NEWSREEL NARRATION
(spoken in German language)
A strange discovery in Egypt... Adventurers unearth the tomb... of King Amen Ho-tep near

Luxor and Thebes. The Mummy and his priests are brought to the surface and see the light of day for the first time in over 4000 years. The mummified remains will be coming soon to a museum near you!

CUT TO BLACK

FADE IN:

Wind rustles through the leaves as the camera cranes down from the trees to reveal a rustic rural rest home nestled in the shade of the East Texas pines.

A Title Card fades up which reads:

Mud Creek, Texas
Present Day

FADE IN:

INTERIOR—REST HOME HALLWAY—DAY
The camera glides down the old dank hallway of the Mud Creek Shady Rest Convalescence Home. Shafts of light streaming in through the transom windows illuminate the stark, empty corridor. The camera smoothly swings around a corner and moves in toward an open door...

DISSOLVE TO:

INTERIOR—REST HOME BEDROOM—DAY
Two FIGURES lie prone in their separate beds, sleeping. Both are old men. The camera moves in on the figure near the window.

ELVIS
(Voice Over)

I was dreamin'... dreamin' my dick was out, and I was checking to see if that infected bump on the head of it had filled with pus again. If it had, I was gonna name that bump after my ex-wife Priscilla, and bust it by jacking off. Or I like

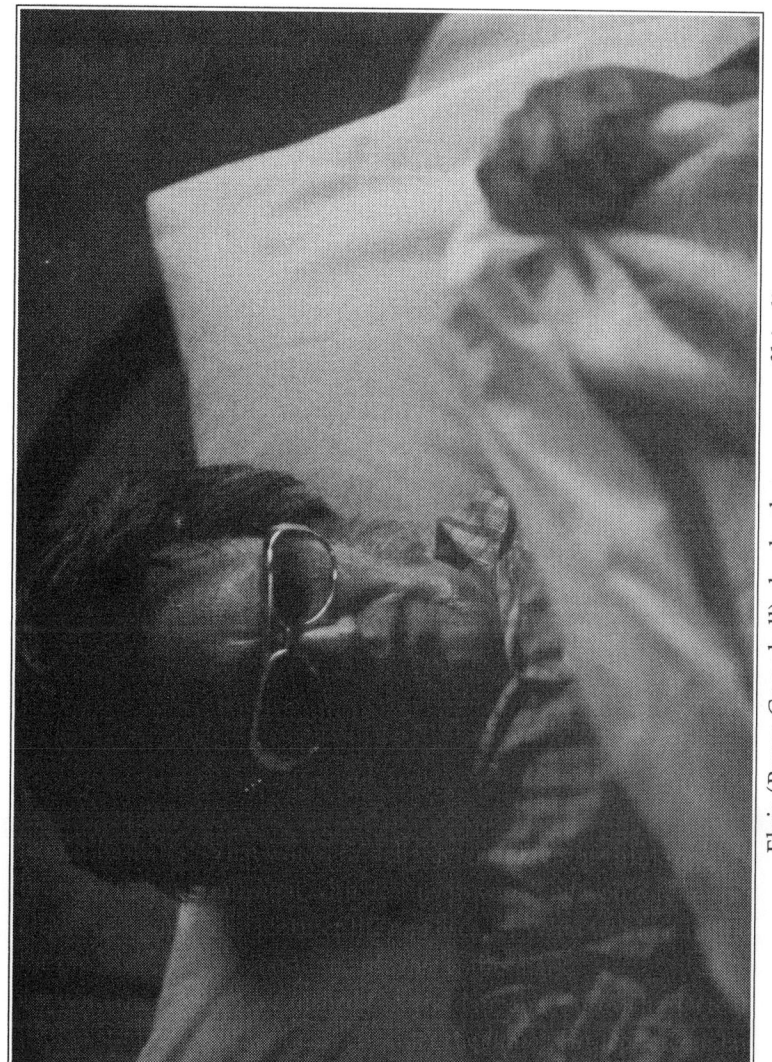

Elvis (Bruce Campbell) checks the progress of his disease.

to think that's what I'd do. Dreams let you think like that. Truth was, I hadn't had a hard-on in years.

AS THE CAMERA MOVES into a CU on the face of an elderly MAN(ELVIS) of some seventy years old, his eyelids begin to flutter as he wakes.

POV—ELVIS—Looking out the door of his room.

The camera is undercranked and the nurses, visitors and residents seem to move by his doorway in fast motion. Elvis considers this surreal image.

From across the room Elvis' roommate, BULL THOMAS, bellows and coughs and moans and falls back into a painful sleep. Elvis reaches over to his bedside table and grabs hold of his thick-rimmed "Elvis-style" GLASSES, puts them on and looks over at Bull.

Elvis takes hold of the bed's LIFT BUTTON and eases himself upright. He glances over at Bull.

Bull is breathing heavily, and his bony knees rise up and down like he is peddling a bicycle; his kneecaps punching feebly at the sheet, making puptents that rise up and collapse, rise up and collapse.

Elvis lays his head back down on the pillow, consumed in thought.

> ELVIS (cont'd)
> (Voice Over)
> My God, man, how long have I been here? Am I really awake now, or am I dreaming I'm awake? How could my plans have gone so wrong? And when the hell are they gonna serve lunch, and considering what they serve, why the hell do I care?

Elvis turns and looks pensively out through the slats of his bedroom window.

>   ELVIS (cont'd)
>   (Voice Over)
>   If Priscilla discovered I was alive, would she come
>   and see me? Would we still want to fuck, or would
>   we merely have to talk about it?

Elvis ponders this deeply.

>   ELVIS (cont'd)
>   (Voice Over)
>   Is there finally, and really, anything to life other
>   than food, shit and sex?

Elvis reaches over, opens his dresser drawer, pulls out a little round mirror and looks at himself.

Elvis is horrified.

>   ELVIS (cont'd)
>   (Voice Over)
>   Well Goddamn it!

We see clearly that his hair is gray and has receded dramatically. He has wrinkles deep enough to conceal outstretched earth worms, the big ones, the night crawlers. His pouty mouth no longer appears pouty.

A sound is heard...of STOMPING FEET—an audience, waiting impatiently for the King...

                                                            CUT TO:

FLASHBACK—STAGE—NIGHT—SLOW MOTION
Elvis is on stage in a black, gold-studded JUMPSUIT. He is forty years old, confident and in command. A pair of women's PANTIES flies through the air and lands at his white boots with a thud.

Elvis (Bruce Campbell) rocks the house.

CUT BACK TO:

Elvis still looks into the mirror. He tries the "curly lip smile" and then drops the mirror in disgust.

>   ELVIS
>   (Voice Over)
> How could I have gone from the King of Rock and Roll to this? Old guy in a rest home in East Texas with a growth on his pecker.

Elvis looks down ominously at the sheet covering him.

>   ELVIS (cont'd)
> And what is that growth? Cancer? Nobody's talking. Nobody seems to know . . . or wants to.

Suddenly, old Bull in the bed next to him gives out, with a hell of a SCREAM, pouching his eyes damn near out of his head and arching his back.

Elvis looks over at his friend. Bull turns his face to Elvis and their EYES LOCK. With pleading eyes, Bull reaches his hand out to Elvis. Sensing Bull's desperation, Elvis leans over and reaches out to him.

Before their hands can touch, Bull takes his last breath and checks his tired old soul out of the Mud Creek Shady Rest Convalescence Home.

Elvis watches with dismay, then lays his head back on his pillow.

CUT TO:

EXTERIOR—REST HOME—DAY
The front wooden DOOR opens and a STRETCHER,(with Bull's corpse under the sheet), is carried out by two ATTENDANTS. As they descend some steps, a sign reads:

> **MUD CREEK SHADY REST**
> **CONVALESCENCE HOME**

Having successfully negotiated the stairs, they move toward the waiting funeral coach.

> ATTENDANT #1
> Makes you wonder, doesn't it? What kind of life this old guy had . . .

> ATTENDANT #2
> Huh?

They roughly slide Bull's corpse into the hearse.

> ATTENDANT #1
> You know, what kind of life he had, the kids, grandkids, the legacy he left . . . and now look at him.

> ATTENDANT #2
> Ahh, who gives a shit.

Attendant #2 slams the hearse door shut.

CUT TO:
INSERT—CU of the tip of a CANE as it taps along the polished linoleum.

INTERIOR—REST HOME HALLWAY—AFTERNOON
ESTHER WAINWRIGHT, eighty years old, with a sweet face and hair so gray it's almost white, works her way down the hall with the aid of her cane.

A MECHANICAL NOISE can be heard up ahead and as she rounds a corner she sees . . .

AN IRON LUNG

with patient inside, the motor below powering a bellows which pumps air into the steel tank.

Esther stops and looks at the iron lung. She cautiously approaches and finds an ELDERLY WOMAN ensconced inside. Esther smiles and the woman smiles back. Esther pats her gently on the head.

Then, she surreptitiously scans the hall. No one is in sight, so, Esther reaches down and gently plucks a pair of gold-rimmed GLASSES, from where they are perched on the woman's face. The woman tries to protest but can only moan her disapproval.

Esther examines the glasses . . . she likes the rhinestones, and then slips them in her pocket and continues walking.

Another Hallway—

Up ahead, Esther spots a GIFT CART left unattended at the end of the hallway. The gift cart is loaded with flowers, magazines, packages, and other items waiting to be delivered to residents.

With anticipation, Esther's cane taps quickly as she moves up to the gift cart and the camera lingers on the object of her affection . . .

A large, yellow, two-pound, TIN OF CHOCOLATES.

Esther scans the area and, seeing that the coast is clear, she filches the candy tin.

CUT TO:

INTERIOR—ESTHER'S BEDROOM—NIGHT
As the camera pans around the dimly-lit bedroom, the outline of a BED, a BUREAU and a CLOSET can be seen. A figure can be seen in the bed, illuminated by a small bedside lamp.

The camera slowly moves in on the bedside table and we see the usual assortment of bedside things(framed PICTURES, pill BOTTLES, knickknacks, etc.) . . .

A NOISE can be heard. A sucking sound . . .

The tin of candy sits on the bedside table.

Esther reaches over and lifts up the lid of the chocolate tin and begins digging around inside. She seizes on an ALMOND CLUSTER and pops the candy into her mouth. Esther begins sucking on her midnight snack... ferociously.

> ESTHER
> Mmmmmm...

Her head sinks back into the pillow as she savors the chocolate, when suddenly...

A NOISE can be heard coming from over near the bedside table.

Esther stops sucking and quizzically looks over in the vicinity of the table. After a moment of consideration, she realizes that...

THE SOUND is coming from the floor.

Esther swallows what's left of her candy and sits up as best she can, craning her neck, searching for the source of the sound.

A CHILL WIND suddenly begins to blow through the thin LACE CURTAINS on her window. She peers over the side of the bed and sees...

SOMETHING scurrying along the floor and under her bed. She quickly looks over to the other side of the bed and sees an insect-like THING, with spidery legs, disappear underneath. She frantically scans the room, but... nothing. The buzzing sound intensifies and Esther whips around to see...

A LUMP in her covers suddenly moves from the foot of her bed rapidly up toward her.

The camera moves in on Esther's face as she clenches her jaw in determination.

                    ESTHER (cont'd)
            . . . gonna squish you, cockroach!

She reaches under the sheet and grabs for the creature. Suddenly, she lets out a bloodcurdling scream and yanks her hand back to reveal . . .

BLOOD covers her hand. It courses down her arm. Recoiling in horror at the sight . . .

Esther loses her balance and tumbles out of the bed, knocking some items off the bedside table. Pulling her sheets with her, Esther lands in a heap on the floor.

Esther regains her senses and notices the outline of the beetle, under the sheets on the floor. She grabs hold of her thick WOODEN CANE and, using it as a weapon, she hauls off and whacks at the form of the creature. Using all her strength, she lays into it and whacks it mercilessly, again and again. Out of breath, and fatigued, Esther drops the cane and scrutinizes . . .

THE MOTIONLESS FORM of the thing under the sheet.

With some trepidation, Esther grabs the end of the sheet and gingerly lifts it to reveal . . .

A big black SCARAB BEETLE, the size of a large fist, sits there, motionless, for a long moment . . . . and then it begins to hiss.

The beetle's HEAD suddenly snaps around, its eyes riveted on Esther. Its little head is black, bug-like and ugly, and it looks severely pissed-off. Just as suddenly the hissing stops. The beetle looks away from Esther, toward the dark corner of the room and the camera racks focus to reveal . . .

AN ILLUSORY FIGURE is silhouetted, rising into our view from the corner of her bedroom. The figure's face cannot be seen but on its head is perched a black, wide-brimmed cowboy HAT.

Esther gasps.

Esther decides to get the hell out. Her fingernails seek purchase on the slick linoleum floor and she begins crawling frantically toward the door.

The figure looms in frame, but all we can make out is the black hat.

Esther frantically drags herself across the floor as we see . . .

Rotten old snakeskin COWBOY BOOTS step into frame and methodically click across the floor in relentless pursuit of the old lady.

Esther reaches the door frame and pulls herself out into the dark, deserted hallway.

CUT TO:

INTERIOR ELVIS' ROOM—NIGHT
Elvis sleeps. A RUSTLING SOUND is heard and he slowly works himself awake. He opens his eyes and looks over toward the source of the sound. Still groggy, he can barely make out . . .

Esther's head on the floor, her fingers grasping his door frame, her face peeking around and up at him, pleading.

Elvis opens his eyes wider as the image registers.

Esther's face mirrors her terror. Trembling with fear, she begins to speak.

ESTHER

    (gasp)
    Help.

Suddenly, without warning, Esther is jerked back out of view by a powerful force.

Elvis blinks, not fully comprehending what he just saw. He puts on his glasses and sees that the floor by his door frame is now empty and everything is quiet once again.

Elvis shrugs, takes off his glassed and lies back on the pillow. He closes his eyes and drifts back to sleep.

CUT TO:

EXTERIOR—REST HOME—DAY
The same two bored Attendants exit the Rest Home carrying Esther's sheet-covered corpse on a stretcher.

> ATTENDANT #1
> You know, I was thinkin'...

> ATTENDANT #2
> I suppose now you're gonna get all weepy on me again.

They drop Esther's corpse into the hearse.

> ATTENDANT #1
> No, I was just going to suggest we throw some deodorizer on the corpse, cause she's smellin' pretty ripe.

> ATTENDANT #2
> Oh, yeah, good idea.

Attendant #2 grabs a can of SPRAY DEODORIZER from the toolkit and begins spraying. After a good coating he kicks the hearse door shut.

CUT TO:

INTERIOR—ELVIS' ROOM—DAY
As sunlight streams in through his bedroom window, Elvis lies sleeping. His eyes drift open and once again we see...

POV—ELVIS—UNDERCRANKED

Out the door of his room. The camera is undercranked and the nurses, visitors and residents seem to move by his doorway in fast motion.

CU—Elvis

Once again, Elvis considers this surreal image. His eyes drift back closed and then suddenly . . .

A NOISE jolts Elvis awake. He rolls over to see . . .

An attractive young WOMAN is cleaning out Bull's dresser DRAWER. The curtains over the window are pulled wide open. The sunlight cuts through it, showing her to great advantage.

She's blonde and is dressed in a somewhat revealing blouse with a short black skirt.

She takes a big, plastic TRASH CAN and with one of Bull's dresser drawers pulled out, she picks through it, like a magpie looking for bright things.

INSERT—DRESSER DRAWER

She finds a few coins, a pocket knife, a cheap watch. These are plucked free and laid on the dresser top.

The remaining contents of the drawer:
—Bull's PHOTOGRAPHS of himself when young—
—a BRONZE STAR and a PURPLE HEART from his performance in the Korean War—
—a tin of chocolates—

These ITEMS are unceremoniously dumped into the trashcan and the lid slaps shut with a bang.

Elvis grabs hold of his bed lift BUTTON and raises himself for a better look.

The woman has her back to him now, and doesn't notice.

She pulls out a drawer full of clothes, takes out the few shirts and pants, socks and underwear, and lays them on Bull's empty bed.

                    ELVIS
Excuse me, Miss. You gonna toss that stuff?

The young woman turns and looks at him.

                  ELVIS (cont'd)
Could I have one of them pictures of Bull? Maybe that Purple Heart? He was pretty proud of it. And that tin of chocolates, maybe?

                YOUNG WOMAN
I suppose ...

She bends over the trashcan and reveals her BLACK PANTIES to Elvis as she rummages.

                    ELVIS
                 (Voice Over)
Lord Almighty ...

Elvis takes a long hard look at her.

                ELVIS (cont'd)
                (Voice Over)
The revealing of her panties was neither intentional or unintentional. She just didn't give a damn. She saw me as so physically and sexually non-threatening, she didn't mind if I got a birds-eye view of her love nest. It was the same to her as a house cat sneaking a peek.

Elvis observes the thin panties straining and slipping into the caverns of her ass cheeks.

>   ELVIS (cont'd)
>   (Voice Over)
>   I felt my pecker flutter once, like a pigeon having a
>   heart attack, then it laid back down and remained
>   limp and still. Well, these days, even a flutter was
>   kind of reassuring . . .

The woman surfaces from the trash can with a PHOTO, the PURPLE HEART MEDAL, and the TIN of candy. She moves over to Elvis' bed and hands them to him.

Elvis dangles the ribbon that holds the Purple Heart between his fingers and considers it.

>   ELVIS (cont'd)
>   Thanks . . . Bull your kin?

>   YOUNG WOMAN
>   My daddy.

>   ELVIS
>   Haven't seen you here before.

>   YOUNG WOMAN
>   Only been here once before. When I checked him in.

>   ELVIS
>   That was three years ago, wasn't it?

>   YOUNG WOMAN
>   (shrugs)
>   You and him friends?

>   ELVIS
>   Just roommates. He didn't feel good enough to say

much. I just sort of hated to see what was left of him go away so easy. He was an all right guy. He mentioned you a lot. You're Callie, right?

                    CALLIE
Yeah, well, he was all right.

                    ELVIS
But not enough so you'd come and see him though . . .

                    CALLIE
Don't try to put some guilt trip on me, mister. I did what I could. Hadn't been for Medicaid, Medicare, whatever that stuff was, he'd been in a ditch somewhere. I sure didn't have the money to take care of him.

Elvis looks away from her, and stares out his window.

                    ELVIS
                (Voice Over)
My own daughter, lost long ago to me. If she knew I lived, would she come to see me? Would she even care?

                ELVIS (cont'd)
You could have come and seen him. They don't charge you for that.

                    CALLIE
Mind your own business. I was busy.

As she zips up her bag and turns away, Elvis looks down at her father's photograph.

INSERT—PHOTO—CU of an old black and white, Korean War-vintage, photograph of a young Bull Thomas, in an Army uniform with a beautiful girl on each arm.

Elvis' NURSE comes into the room. She smiles at Callie and then at Elvis.

> NURSE
> How are you this morning, Mr. Haff?

> ELVIS
> All right, but I prefer "Mr. Presley". Or "Elvis". I keep telling you that. I don't go by "Sebastian Haff" anymore. I don't try to hide anymore.

> NURSE
> Why, of course, I knew that. I forgot. Good morning, "Elvis".

Her voice drips sarcastically with sorghum syrup.

Elvis glares at her, as if he'd be happy to wop her in the head with his bed pan.

The nurse turns to Callie...

> NURSE (cont'd)
> Did you know we have a celebrity here, Miss Thomas? Elvis Presley. You know, the rock and roll singer?

> CALLIE
> I thought he was dead.

Callie moves back to the dresser, squats, and sets to work on the bottom drawer. The nurse looks at Elvis and smiles again, only she speaks to Callie.

> NURSE
> Well, actually, Elvis is dead, and Mr. Haff knows that, don't you, Mr. Haff?

ELVIS
Hell no. I'm right here. I ain't dead . . . yet.

NURSE
Now, Mr. Haff, I don't mind calling you Elvis, but you're a little confused, or like to play sometimes. You were an Elvis impersonator. Remember? You fell off a stage and broke your hip. What was it . . . twenty years ago? It got infected and you were in a coma for quite awhile. You came out with a few . . .

The Nurse looks over at Callie.

NURSE (cont'd)
. . . problems.

ELVIS
I was just impersonating myself. I couldn't do nothin' else. I haven't got any problems. You're trying to say my brain is messed up, aren't you?

Callie quits cleaning out the bottom drawer of the dresser. She's interested now.

CALLIE
For an old fella, you seem pretty sharp to me. But I don't understand why . . . why would you want to be somebody else?

ELVIS
(the camera begins to move in on Elvis)
I got tired of it. I got hooked on pills, you know. I wanted out. Fella named Sebastian Haff, an Elvis imitator, the best of 'em, he took my place. But he had a bad heart and he liked drugs too. Liked 'em more than I did. It was him died, not me. I just took his place.

DISSOLVE TO:
EXTERIOR—RURAL HIGHWAY—DAY—FLASHBACK
A shiny black CADILLAC LIMO hurtles down the highway toward a shimmering red SUNSET.

> CALLIE
> (Distant, Echoey Voice Over)
> But why would you want to leave all that fame, Mr. Presley? All that money?
> (Her voice echoes away)

INTERIOR—CADILLAC LIMO—DAY
Inside the Caddy, Elvis sits brooding in the back seat. Sideburns . . . sunglasses . . . 42 years old. The car is loaded with Elvis' "boys".

> ELVIS
> (Voice Over)
> Cause it got old. Woman I loved, Priscilla, she was gone. Rest of the women . . . were just women. The music wasn't mine anymore. I wasn't even me anymore, just this thing they made up. And my "friends" . . . they were suckin' me dry.

Elvis looks around at his "Boys" and in a slow motion effect they laugh and carry on.

EXTERIOR—RURAL HIGHWAY—DAY
The Cadillac limo screams past a sign:

NACOGDOCHES HARVEST CARNIVAL

> ELVIS
> (Voice Over)
> So I took a little road trip down to Nacogdoches . . . to check out this . . . Sebastian Haff.

CUT TO:
EXTERIOR—REAR OF HIGH SCHOOL GYMNASIUM—DAY

The Cadillac skids to a stop behind a dilapidated country high school gymnasium. The HARVEST CARNIVAL can be seen out on the field in the distance. Noise and music can be heard. A few PEOPLE are walking toward it.

Elvis' Boys clamber out of the caddy, scan the area to make sure the coast is clear. They open the door and Elvis emerges.

SLOW MOTION—ELVIS, surrounded by his retinue, strides across the parking lot.

They enter the gym's rear door.

CUT TO:

INTERIOR—LOCKER ROOM HALLWAY—DAY
The entourage leads the way down a dank, dimly-lit locker room hallway. They stop at a door with a crude sign taped to it which reads:

SEBASTIAN HAFF
Do Not Disturb

Elvis motions for his boys to stop.

ELVIS
You boys wait here.

Elvis opens the door and enters the room.

CUT TO:

INTERIOR—GYM LOCKER/DRESSING ROOM—DAY
Seated at a card table in the corner with his back to Elvis, SEBASTIAN HAFF is chowing down on a large piece of blueberry PIE. Dressed in a blue, studded jumpsuit, Sebastian suddenly senses Elvis' presence and swivels around in his chair.

Sebastian is a good one, looks identical, maybe a shade too much gut. Cool as he is, Sebastian starts to lose it.

                    SEBASTIAN HAFF
            Oh my Gawd . . . I never thought you'd really . . .

He nervously wipes his face with a napkin, then shuffles forward and drops to his knees before Elvis.

The real KING extends a hand and Sebastian plants a kiss on one of those big gold rings.

CUT TO:
INTERIOR—LOCKER ROOM HALLWAY—DAY
Elvis' boys are milling in the hall when the door swings open and "Elvis" exits, pulling up the collar of his black leather jacket. He hesitates for a moment and then . . .

                          "ELVIS"
            (hoarse whisper)
            Just another freak. Let's split, boys.

"ELVIS" wipes some blueberry pie off the corner of his mouth and charges down the hallway with his boys following behind.

                                                    CUT TO:
EXTERIOR—GYMNASIUM—EVENING
The Cadillac limousine sits idling nearby as they exit the gym. "Elvis" starts to reach for the rear door handle when . . .

One of his Boys grabs it first and opens the door for the King.

                          DRIVER
            Woow now, King.

A sly smile appears on the face of "Elvis" as he gets into the car.

                          "ELVIS"
            It's all yours, baby.

Elvis (Bruce Campbell) decides to switch places with an impersonator in "Bubba Ho-Tep".

The boys pile in, the doors swing shut and the Caddy tears off in a cloud of dust.

THE CAMERA PANS
around to reveal the real Elvis, now dressed in Sebastian's blue jumpsuit, watching the car disappear from the doorway. He has exchanged places with his impersonator, Sebastian Haff.

> ELVIS
> (Voice Over)
> I left all the money with Sebastian, 'cept for enough to sustain me if things got bad. I was determined to make myself a new life . . . a better one.

CUT TO:

EXTERIOR—TRAILER PARK—DAY
CU on a small smoky Barbecue. Burgers and dogs are roasting over the fire. A small, shabby old Airstream sits parked in a quiet rural trailer park.

Elvis flips the burgers and dogs, then grabs hold of a CAN of lighter fluid and squirts it into the fire. A plume of flame roils up and Elvis backs away from the heat.

> ELVIS
> (Voice Over)
> But me and Sebastian, we had us a deal. If I wanted to trade back, he'd let me. It was all written up in a contract.

He sets down the can of lighter fluid and (unknown to him) it tips over.

> TRAILER PARK DUDE
> Yo, Sebastian!!

Elvis leaves the barbecue . . .

ELVIS
(Voice Over)
Thing was, I lost my copy in a barbecue accident.

Elvis saunters over to a PICNIC BENCH where some Trailer Park Trash-type NEIGHBORS are sitting.

ELVIS (cont'd)
(Voice Over)
But that wasn't so bad either. I was makin' new friends and enjoying myself.

One of the girls offers him a CAN of beer. Elvis takes the beer, flips the pop-top and they toast.

Suddenly, with a bang, a huge FIREBALL erupts from Elvis' trailer as it spontaneously bursts into flame.

Elvis spins around to see his trailer and the one next to it explode into a fiery inferno.

NURSE
(Voice over)
Now, Elvis. Don't carry it too far...

The flashback ends as we—

DISSOLVE BACK TO:

INTERIOR—ELVIS' ROOM—DAY

Elvis shakes himself out of his daydream. He looks up to see the Nurse and Callie still at his bedside.

NURSE (Cont'd)
You may just get way out there and not come back.

Elvis surveys his grim reality.

ELVIS
Oh fuck you.

The Nurse starts to giggle.

> ELVIS (cont'd)
> (to himself)
> Shit. Get old, you can't even cuss somebody and have it bother 'em. Everything you do is either worthless . . . or sadly amusing.

The women smile at one another, passing a private joke.

> CALLIE
> I've got what I want.

She scrapes the bright things off the top of Bull's dresser and into her purse.

> CALLIE (cont'd)
> The clothes can go to Goodwill or the Salvation Army.

The nurse nods to Callie.

> NURSE
> Very well. And I'm very sorry about your father. He was a nice man.

> CALLIE
> Yeah.

She pauses at the foot of Elvis' bed.

> CALLIE (cont'd)
> Nice to meet you, Mr. Presley.

> ELVIS
> Get the hell out.

> NURSE
> Now, now . . .

She pats his foot through the covers, as if it were a little cantankerous dog.

> NURSE (CONT'D)
> I'll be back later to do that . . . little "thing" . . . that has to be done. You know.

Callie and the Nurse move out of the room, and down the hall, punishing him with the clean lines of their faces and the sheen of their hair, the jiggle of their asses and tits. Elvis can hear them laughing at him from down the hall.

Elvis picks up Bull's purple heart medal and considers it.

> ELVIS
> (to himself)
> Poor Bull. In the end, does anything really matter?

Elvis sinks his head back into the pillow and closes his eyes, fighting back tears.

> ELVIS (cont'd)
> (Voice Over)
> Nobody around here ever believed me . . . cept for this one guy . . . only he was certifiable.

FLASHBACK TO:
EXT—REST HOME—DAY—FLASHBACK
On the tree-shrouded lawn, Jack, an elderly black man in his seventies, sits in his wheelchair beside Elvis. Both men have blankets on their laps. Jack points to the back of his head.

> JACK
> That's where they took that piece of my brain out. They got it back in D.C . . . in that goddamn jar. I got a little bag of sand up there now . . .

                    ELVIS
        Jack, no offense, but President Kennedy was a white
        man.

                     JACK
        That's how clever they are. They dyed me this color.

Jack leans in close to Elvis in a conspiratorial fashion.

                 JACK (cont'd)
                   (whispers)
        Can you think of a better way to hide the truth than
        that??

CUT BACK TO:
EXTERIOR—REST HOME—NIGHT
Establishing shot of the Mud Creek Shady Rest bathed in moonlight.

CUT TO:
INTERIOR—ELVIS' ROOM—NIGHT
Elvis is in bed sleeping. He thrashes around . . . mumbling . . . dreaming and we . . .

CUT TO:
EXTERIOR—DESERT HIGHWAY—DAY
CU on the wide chrome grille of a Cadillac.

We pull back to reveal a maroon Cadillac convertible screaming down the highway with Elvis(at age 43), by himself, at the wheel. Elvis is dressed casual, polyester shirt and pants.

                    ELVIS
                  (Voice Over)
        . . . but I was living simple. The way Haff had been.

Elvis checks the time by flipping down the window VISOR to reveal an OLD WATCH taped on the underside of the visor.

                    ELVIS (cont'd)
          Going from town to town doing the Elvis act.
          Only I felt like I was really me again. Can you dig
          that?

A RUMBLING SOUND fades up as we:

SUPERIMPOSE: THE NURSE AND CALLIE stand over Elvis' bed (as part of this dream sequence), listening to him intently as he spins his yarn.

                         NURSE
          We're digging it, Mr. Haff . . . Mr. Presley.

The rumbling sound continues until we realize it is the opening notes of Elvis' tradition opening musical introduction . . .

                                                  CUT TO:
EXTERIOR—STAGE AT COUNTY FAIR—NIGHT
Searchlights sweep the small crowd as they cheer in anticipation of the arrival of "Elvis". As the music crescendos, all searchlights hit the stage . . .

The curtains fly open and "Sebastian Haff" takes the stage in front of a small county fair crowd of mostly older folk.

A pounding rock beat builds.

INSERT—BASS DRUM

As the pounding beat intensifies we can read the front skin of the Bass drum:

                   SEBASTIAN HAFF
                  "A tribute to the KING"

ELVIS' ROCK BAND kicks into a potent rock vamp.

"Sebastian" charges to the edge of the stage strikes a pose and then suddenly whips through a cool routine of Elvis' patented Karate chops.

In the front row, four or five "screamers", women well into middle-age fawn over his performance.

> ELVIS
> (Voice Over)
> Women throwing themselves at me, 'cause they could imagine I was Elvis, only I was Elvis, playing Sebastian Haff... playing Elvis... It was all pretty good. I didn't mind the contract being burned up. I didn't even try to go back and convince anybody. Then I had the accident.

"Sebastian" is really getting into it...

> ELVIS (cont'd)
> (Voice Over)
> I was gyratin' ya see, takin' care of business, but then my hip went out. I'd been having trouble with it...

ELVIS' HIP goes out with a crack and he topples off the edge of the stage.

IN SLOW MOTION—ELVIS falls headfirst into the empty orchestra pit. He plummets straight toward the concrete.

Upon impact, a CONCUSSIVE SOUND is heard as we...

CUT TO BLACK

CUT BACK TO:

INT. ELVIS' ROOM—NIGHT
Elvis stirs awake, groggily comes to and lifts himself up on one elbow. He shakes the cobwebs out of his mind.

                    ELVIS
          (mutters)
          Damn, it's cold in here tonight.

Elvis reaches around, grabs hold of his METAL BED PAN, and studies it.

                    ELVIS (cont'd)
          All right. This time I make it. No more piss or crap
          in the bed.

Elvis sits up and hangs his feet off the side of the bed. As the dizziness passes, Elvis looks at his WALKER waiting beside his bed. He sighs, slips on his ROBE, leans forward, takes hold of the grips and eases himself off the bed. He reaches down and flips on his OLD ELECTRIC FLOOR HEATER.

The exposed ELECTRIC COILS quickly GLOW RED giving the room an eerie illumination.

Elvis clumps the rubber-padded tips of the walker forward, and makes for the toilet.

                                                          CUT TO:
INTERIOR—BATHROOM—NIGHT
Elvis is urinating. He is about to flush the toilet when he hesitates . . . hearing something out in the darkness of the room.

POV—DARK BEDROOM

A soft scratching is heard as the camera pans his dark bedroom.

INTERIOR—ELVIS' ROOM—NIGHT
A chill WIND suddenly begins to blow through the thin lace CURTAINS on his window.

Elvis peers around the room but nothing seems to be out of place.

Elvis slowly thumps the walker back toward his bed. As he is about to sit down, Elvis suddenly notices on the floor . . .

POV—Upside down tin of chocolates—with candies scattered about.

A scratching sound emanates from underneath the chocolate tin. The tin shimmies and then jerks.

Elvis reaches over and takes hold of the tin's lid. He slowly lifts it to reveal . . .

The black SCARAB BEETLE. The same one that killed old Esther.

The BEETLE'S HEAD suddenly snaps around and its eyes lock on Elvis.

Elvis stares at the creature and whistles in amazement.

                            ELVIS
    Wooow. You are one big bitch cockroach . . .

The beetle hisses a response and, without warning, springs toward Elvis' face.

The King's reflexes are a bit sharper than Esther's were. He manages to duck as the big bug buzzes over his head, missing him by a hair. Elvis tumbles to the ground and his glasses slide across the floor. Flat on the floor, Elvis manages to get his bearings and grab hold of his walker. He grabs his glasses and pulls himself to his feet, scanning the room.

He sees nothing . . . then from behind him, he can hear a SCUTTLING SOUND. Behind him, on the far wall, the scarab can be seen scurrying upward. Elvis senses its presence and whips around to face it.

The bug rotates on the wall and stops . . . and then, it's ugly head pops out and looks at him.

Elvis recoils for an instant but then, just as quickly, responds forcefully to the bug's challenging glare.

Elvis whips through a couple of his signature Karate chops and challenges right back.

>   ELVIS (cont'd)
>   Alright man, let's go.

For a moment it's a standoff... as they just stare at one another... until Elvis notices his DINNER TRAY, and a large, sharp-tined FORK, resting beside him on Bull's bed. Without taking his eyes off the beetle, Elvis reaches for the tray, grabs the implement and hoists it up, wielding it as a weapon... until he realizes he is holding a SPOON.

Elvis curses and drops the spoon, when suddenly...

The scarab beetle's elytra retract and a set of gossamer wings snap out. With a shrieking battle cry, the scarab launches itself off the wall and dive bombs toward Elvis' head. Elvis ducks as the bug buzzes him.

>   ELVIS (cont'd)
>   Hot damn!

The scarab makes a series of dive bomb runs as Elvis jerks up his walker and tries to fend off the crazed creature.

The scarab comes to a stop and hovers menacingly in front of Elvis, wings beating ferociously.

Elvis scans the room, examining his options, searching for a weapon. He spots his metal bedpan on the bed.

The scarab beetle, rears back and then, wings spinning like helicopter rotors, screams in on a kamikaze flight path aiming directly for Elvis' head.

POV—SCARAB BEETLE as the evil insect barrels in on Elvis.

Elvis manages to jerk up the bedpan, just an instant before impact, and...

The scarab beetle slams into the metal pan and Elvis drives it into the wall... trapping the bug.

> ELVIS (cont'd)
> Gotcha! You six-legged bastard!

Elvis is elated at capturing the creature, but then notices that the room is silent... there is no sound coming from beneath the bedpan. Elvis gently pulls the bedpan from off the wall and then turns, not certain where the bug has gone. Then he senses something and flips over the bedpan to reveal...

The BEETLE is clinging inside. Before he can react, the scarab lunges for his face.

Elvis instinctively recoils, loses his balance and topples over, flopping flat onto the floor, stunned.

CU Elvis as he shakes his head and opens his eyes to see...

The scarab beetle is across the room, on the floor and is motorvating... legs working overtime... scrambling across the tile, heading straight toward his face.

The relentless scarab beetle skitters at full speed toward Elvis.

Elvis gulps loudly as the gravity of his predicament registers. He frantically reaches around behind himself, trying to find that bedpan... anything to ward off this nemesis.

INSERT—DINNER FORK

Elvis' fingers wrap around the handle of the stainless-steel utensil.

As the beetle zeros in on his face, with all his strength, Elvis hoists his newfound weapon and . . .

HE RAMS THE FORK directly into the Scarab Beetle's thorax, impaling it to the floor.

Elvis yanks the creature up off the floor and examines the stuck bug.

The scarab beetle struggles furiously but is unable to extricate itself from the impalement. A greenish fluid oozes out of its wound.

Elvis eyes the creature's predicament with satisfaction.

     ELVIS (cont'd)
 Even a big bitch cockroach like you should know . . .
 never, but never . . . fuck with the King.

Elvis shoves the beetle through the protective grill and into the glowing coils of the nearby floor heater.

The creature shrieks in agony as the hot voltage surges through its body.

The electrocuted beetle bursts into flame and is quickly incinerated.

Elvis pulls the fork out from the coils with the remnants of the flaming beetle and, like with a burning marshmallow, he blows it out.

             CUT TO:

INTERIOR—HALLWAY—NIGHT
As smoke wafts out of Elvis' room, he clumps out with his walker. The hallway is semidark, with every other light cut, and the lights that are on dimmed to a watery egg-yoke yellow.

      ELVIS
 Hey . . . anybody out here?

As his voice echoes down the hallway, Elvis listens, but there is no response.

>   ELVIS (cont'd)
> I think we got us a major bug problem in this place.

Elvis looks in either direction, seeing no one. Then he hesitates, hearing something down the hallway.

A kind of SCRAMBLING NOISE is heard—like a big spider scuttling about in a box of gravel.

Elvis swings the walker forward and moves in the direction of the noise.

Elvis clumps on down the dark, empty hall. Up ahead, he spots an open door.

INTERIOR—JACK'S ROOM—NIGHT
Elvis pokes his head inside and peers into Jack's room and sees . . . a room much different than his. Featuring cream-colored walls and plush blue carpet the room is packed with books, little luxuries, and even a fancy electric WHEELCHAIR. Next to Jack's bed is a miniature diorama of Dealy Plaza, and figurines of JFK, his limo and Oswald in the miniature window of the Texas Book Depository.

Elvis sees that the four-poster bed is empty, and then notices a FIGURE (JACK), lying slumped on the floor, behind the desk.

>   ELVIS
> (mutters)
> Whoa, man?!

Elvis clumps into the room, positions his walker next to Jack, takes a deep breath and steps out of it, supporting himself with one side of it. He gets down on his knees beside him. Jack is still breathing. Elvis notices . . .

A SCAR at Jack's hairline. A long scar that makes Jack's skin lighter there, almost gray.

                    ELVIS (cont'd)
          (mutters)
          What the Sam Hill???

Elvis reaches out to touch the scar and then grabs him by the shoulder.

                    ELVIS (cont'd)
          Jack. Man, you okay?

No response. Elvis thinks for a moment, shrugs and then . . .

                    ELVIS (cont'd)
          Mr. Kennedy.

Jack begins to stir, opens his eyes and looks up.

                    JACK
          Uh . . .

                    ELVIS
          Hey, man. You're on the floor.

                    JACK
          No shit. Who are you?

Elvis hesitates. He is about to say "Elvis", then thinks better of it.

                    ELVIS
          Sebastian . . . .Sebastian Haff.

Elvis takes hold of Jack's shoulder and rolls him over. Jack lies on his back now. He strays an eyeball at Elvis. He starts to speak, hesitates. Jack finally gets his breath.

                         JACK
           Did you see him go by in the hall?

Elvis just looks at him.

                      JACK (cont'd)
           He scuttled like.

                         ELVIS
           Who, man?

                         JACK
           Someone they sent.

                         ELVIS
           Who's they?

                         JACK
           Oh, you know who.

Jack sits up, still wild-eyed.

                         ELVIS
           No, Jack, I don't.

                         JACK
           Lyndon Johnson. Castro, maybe. They've sent
           someone to finish me off. I think maybe it was
           Johnson himself. Real ugly. Real goddamn ugly.

                         ELVIS
           President Johnson's dead.

                         JACK
           That won't stop him.

                                                    CUT TO:

INTERIOR—JACK'S ROOM—NIGHT

A team of NURSES circles around Jack. They lift him back into bed. On the other side of the room . . .

The bespectacled HOSPITAL ADMINISTRATOR interrogates Elvis.

          ADMINISTRATOR
You say you heard a noise?

          ELVIS
Yeah well I was following a sound . . . I mean I heard something. It was like a . . . "scuttling".

          ADMINISTRATOR
A scuttling sound. Were you awake or were you in bed when you heard this noise?

          ELVIS
Well, I was in bed first and then I was awake . . . because the damn bugs woke me up. You got bugs all over this place.

          ADMINISTRATOR
Bugs. Well Mr. Haff, what kind of bugs have you been seeing?

          ELVIS
Do I look like an icthyologist? Big damn bugs . . . the size of your fist . . . the size of a peanut butter and banana sandwich. What do I care, I've got a growth on my pecker.

          ADMINISTRATOR
Okay, Mr. Haff. Don't worry about a thing. We'll call the exterminator tomorrow and we'll take care of the problem.

          ELVIS
Thank you. Thank you very much.

DISSOLVE TO:

EXTERIOR—REST HOME—DAY
Establishing shot of the peaceful Mud Creek Shady Rest Convalescence Home, wedged in the East Texas pines, bathed in the morning sunlight.

CUT TO:

INTERIOR—ELVIS' ROOM—DAY
Later that morning, sunlight shoots into Elvis' room through the Venetian blinds. With a loud snap, Elvis' nurse pulls on a set of LATEX GLOVES and grasps a JAR of salve.

>   NURSE
> Time for that "little thing" again.

CU on the nurse as she pulls back Elvis' sheets and takes hold of his pitiful little pecker in her gloved hands. She begins putting salve on his canker with all the enthusiasm of a mechanic oiling a defective part.

Elvis, depressed, shakes his head.

>   ELVIS
>   (thinking to himself)
> A doll like this, handlin' me without warmth or
> emotion... Twenty years ago, just twenty... I
> could have made with the curly lip smile and had
> her eatin' out of my asshole.

The Nurse continues working his member.

>   NURSE
> Doctor says this cream ought to do the trick... corticosteroids... should heal the inflammation and stop the pus.

Elvis ignores her, lost in thought.

ELVIS
                 (Voice Over)
Where'd my youth go? Why didn't fame hold off
old age and death, and why the hell did I leave the
fame in the first place, and do I want it back, and
could I have it back, and if I could, would it make
any difference?

As the camera moves in on his face . . . he considers the events of the
night before.

                                      FLASHBACK TO:
Montage of fast cuts—
—The SCARAB BEETLE flying through the air
—The BEDPAN swings through the air
—Elvis stabs the scarab with the FORK
—Jack is put to bed by the nurses
—Bull's daughter leans into the TRASH CAN

                                        CUT BACK TO:
INTERIOR—ELVIS' ROOM—DAY
Elvis is still daydreaming, so wrapped up in these considerations, he
has lost awareness of the nurse until . . .

                    NURSE
    Mr. Haff.

                    ELVIS
    (slightly startled)
    Huh?

Elvis notices that she is smiling and looking down at her hands. He
looks down there too.

                 ELVIS (cont'd)
                 (Voice Over)
    Lord Almighty . . .

NURSE
You ole' rascal. I think you better take a cold shower, Mr. Haff.

A sly grin creeps up over Elvis' countenance.

ELVIS
(Voice Over)
There'd been two presidential elections since I'd had a boner like that one. What gave here? Then I realized what gave. I was thinking about things that interested me, not my next meal or goin' to the crapper. I'd been given a dose of life again.

Elvis looks up at her with a Cheshire cat grin.

ELVIS (cont'd)
You get in there with me, I'll take that shower.

NURSE
You silly thing . . .

The Nurse removes her plastic gloves with a snap and drops them in the trash can beside his bed.

ELVIS
Why don't you pull on it a little.

She grabs hold of his night gown, pulls it down and throws his sheet over him.

NURSE
You ought to be ashamed.

The Nurse turns and exits the room, shaking her head.

Elvis looks down at the bulge in his covers, lifts the blankets and takes a peek. A satisfied smile appears on Elvis' face as he leans back and folds his arms behind his head.

CUT TO:

INTERIOR—SHADY GROVE LUNCH ROOM—LUNCHTIME
Elvis sits staring at a PLATE of steamed green beans and broccoli and a baloney sandwich on a tray in front of him. A dry roll, a pat of butter and a short glass of milk soldiered on the side. It is not inspiring. In the corner, a blue-haired old GAL picks her way through an old song on a dusty Hammond Organ.

An OLD MAN wearing a BLACK MASK and a WHITE STETSON, known to residents and staff alike as "KEMOSABE", snaps one of his two capless CAP PISTOLS in the air muttering to himself.

> KEMOSABE
> Under the bridge... I saw him under the bridge... it's an ambush!! My boots, Tonto, my boots!

> ELVIS
> (Voice Over)
> That's my friend, Kemosabe. We used to play cards together. Now, he doesn't even know who I am.

Elvis takes his dinner fork, hefts it like a weapon, as he remembers the previous night's events.

Elvis looks up and glances down the length of the table to see... Jack Kennedy.

Elvis catches the old man looking at him, as if they shared a secret. Elvis smiles back, then frowns and looks away.

CUT TO:

INTERIOR—ELVIS' ROOM—NIGHT
The camera moves in on Elvis in a deep sleep. Suddenly he awakes with a start and turns his head toward the intrusion.

In the doorway is the silhouetted figure of a YOUNG WOMAN.

Elvis, still groggy, tries to force himself awake as he stares at the figure. The figure calls to him, plaintively.

                    FIGURE
   (whispers)
   Daddy?

Elvis shakes his head.

                    ELVIS
   Baby?

CU Elvis as he peers intently at the door.

Suddenly we see that Jack stands next to the bed, looking down at Elvis.

The doorway is empty, the young woman is gone.

Jack is wearing a suit coat over his pajamas and he has on thick glasses.

                    JACK
   Sebastian. It's loose.

Elvis collects his thoughts and pastes them together into a not too scattered collage.

                    ELVIS
   What's loose?

                    JACK
   It . . . listen.

Elvis listens.

Out in the hall he hears . . .

The SCUTTLING SOUND of the night before.

> ELVIS
>
> Jesus Christ, what's that?

> JACK
>
> I thought it was Lyndon Johnson, but I've come across new evidence that suggests another assassin.

> ELVIS
>
> Assassin?

Jack cocks an ear. The sound has gone away, moved distant, then ceases.

> JACK
>
> It's got another target tonight. Come on. I want to show you something. I don't think it's safe if you go back to sleeping.

> ELVIS
>
> For chrissake . . . tell the administrators.

> JACK
>
> The suits and white starches? No thank you. I trusted them back when I was in Dallas, and look where that got my brain and me. I'm thinking with sand up here, maybe picking up a few waves from my brain. Someday, who's to say they won't just disconnect the battery at the White House?

> ELVIS
>
> Oh that's something to worry about, all right . . .

> JACK
>
> Listen here, I know you're Elvis.

Jack stares coldly and directly into Elvis' eyes.

> JACK (cont'd)
> There were rumors, you know... about how you hated me, but I've thought it over. You hated me, you could have finished me off the other night.

Elvis raises up on one elbow and considers the implications.

> JACK (cont'd)
> All I want from you is to look me straight in the eye and assure me you had nothing to do with that day in Dallas, and that you never knew Lee Harvey Oswald or Jack Ruby.

Elvis swings his legs over the side of the bed and sits up. He stares at Jack as sincerely as possible.

> ELVIS
> I had nothing to do with Dallas, and I knew neither Lee Harvey Oswald nor Jack Ruby.

> JACK
> Good. May I call you Elvis instead of Sebastian?

> ELVIS
> You may.

> JACK
> Excellent. You wear glasses to read?

> ELVIS
> I wear glasses when I really want to see.

> JACK
> Then get 'em and come on.

Jack jumps to his feet and charges out the door.

CUT TO:

INTERIOR—HALLWAY—NIGHT
Elvis clumps his walker down the hallway with Jack on crutches beside him. Both wear their GLASSES.

>   ELVIS
>   (Voice Over)
>   The walker swung along easily tonight. Damn, this
>   Jack's a nut . . . and maybe I'm nuts too, but there's
>   an adventure going on . . .

They come to a stop in front of the hall rest room. The one reserved for male visitors.

>   JACK
>   In here.

They move into the rest room.

INTERIOR—REST ROOM—NIGHT
The old tile rest room is large and empty, with several stalls and urinals.

>   JACK
>   Over here.

Jack moves over to one of the stalls and pushes open the door and stands back by the commode to make room for Elvis' walker.

Elvis eases inside and looks at what Jack is now pointing to.

On the bathroom wall appears to be some GRAFFITI.

>   ELVIS
>   That's it? We're investigating a scuttling in the hall,
>   trying to discover who attacked you last night, and
>   you bring me in here to show me stick pictures on
>   the shit house wall?

Screenplay by Don Coscarelli

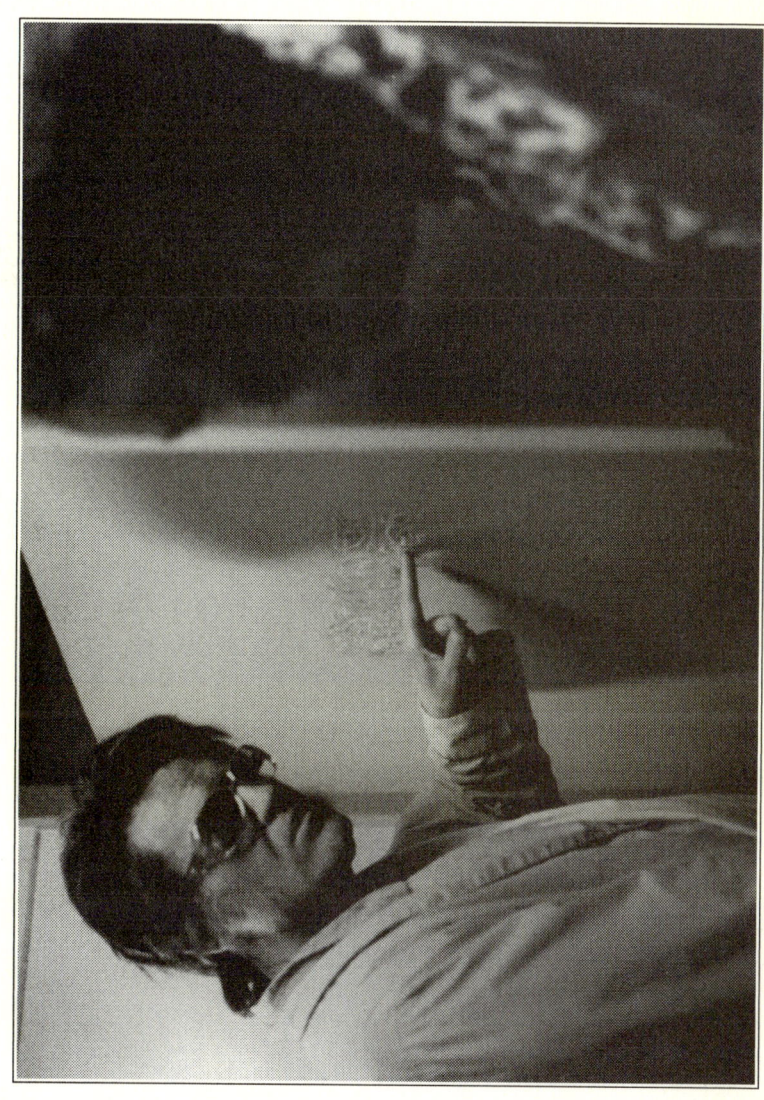

Elvis (Bruce Campbell) and JFK (Ossie Davis) investigate the mystery of Bubba Ho-Tep.

                        JACK
    Look close.

Elvis leans forward. His eyes aren't what they used to be and his
glasses probably need to be upgraded, but he can see that instead of
writing, the graffiti is a series of simple pictorials.

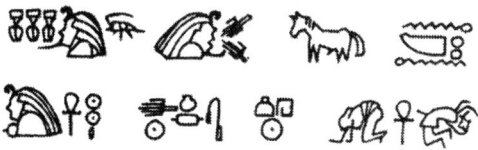

                        ELVIS
    It's Egyptian...

                        JACK
    Right-a-reen-o. Hey, you're not as stupid as some
    folks made you out.

                        ELVIS
    Thanks.

Jack reaches into his suit coat pocket and takes out a folded piece of
PAPER and unfolds it. He presses it to the wall.

Elvis sees that it is covered with the same sort of figures that are on
the wall of the toilet stall.

                        JACK
    I copied this down yesterday. Came in here to shit
    because they hadn't cleaned up my bathroom. I saw
    this on the wall, went back to my room, looked it
    up in my books and wrote it all down. The top line
    translates roughly to something like: "Pharaoh
    gobbles donkey goobers." And the bottom line is:
    "Cleopatra does the nasty."

                        ELVIS
    What?

                          JACK
    Well, pretty much . . . that's the best I can translate.

Elvis is mystified.

                          ELVIS
    All right, so one of the nuts in here, present company excluded, thinks he's Tutankhamun or something, and he writes on the wall in hieroglyphics. So what? I mean, what's the connection? Why are we hanging out in a toilet?

                          JACK
    I don't know how they connect exactly. Not yet. But this . . . thing, it caught me asleep last night, and I came awake just in time to . . . well, he had me on the floor and had his mouth over my asshole.

                          ELVIS
    (horrified)
    A shit eater?

                          JACK
    I don't think so. He was after my soul. You can get that out of any of the major orifices in a person's body. I've read about it.

                          ELVIS
    Where? Hustler?

                          JACK
    "The Everyday Man or Woman's Book of the Soul" by David Webb. It has some pretty good movie reviews about stolen soul movies in the back too. Come on, I'll show you.

Jack turns and makes his way out of the rest room and Elvis shakes his head in dismay.

CUT TO:

EXTERIOR—SIDE PORCH OF REST HOME—NIGHT
ECU—a match is struck, flares and Elvis' nurse brings it up to her face, lighting a cigarette.

Wider shot—The nurse stands on the side porch of the rest home and takes a drag off the cigarette.

A NOISE is heard from around the corner . . . is it a whimpering??

The nurse turns in the direction of the noise. She listens intently and then slowly moves down the porch steps.

At the corner of the building she leans out and looks toward the GARDENER'S SHED, about 30 feet away. The shed door is ajar.

A light inside the shed can be seen strobing on and off.

The nurse takes a step toward the shed, thinks better of it, turns back to the porch and . . .

The nurse bumps into the Administrator who stands right behind her.

Startled, the nurse catches her breath.

>   NURSE
> (recovering)
> There's a light shorting out in the gardener's shed.

>   ADMINISTRATOR
> This whole place is falling apart. Just forget it. Mrs. Biddlesteen is waiting for her enema.

>   NURSE
> Alright, alright . . . I'm coming . . . just let me finish my cigarette.

The nurse takes a drag off her cigarette as the administrator exits.

MYSTERIOUS POV—from shed watching the nurse. Treated with a strange effect(we'll call this "Mummyvision").

The nurse looks over her shoulder suspiciously at the shed. She takes a last drag off of her cigarette, drops it to the ground and crushes it out under her heel. She exits.

At the Gardener's Shed—Low Angle(almost on the floor)—the shed door slowly swings open and, illuminated by the strobing light, we see A BODY of an old resident sprawled on the floor. A wheelchair is tipped on its side nearby with one wheel still slowly turning.

A SNAKESKIN COWBOY BOOT steps out over the body.

CUT TO:

INTERIOR—JACK'S ROOM—NIGHT
Back in Jack's room, Elvis sits on his bed, thumbing through his many books on astrology, the Kennedy assassination, and a number of other esoteric tomes.

Elvis opens a page to reveal:

**The Everyday Man or Woman's
Book of the Soul**

He flips through the book with fascination.

INSERT—BOOK

He flips through the graphically illustrated pages with subject headings such as:

SOUL SUCKERS

STEALING SOULS

VAMPIRES AND GHOULS

SUCCUBI AND INCUBI

Elvis reads slowly while Jack heats hot water with his plug-in HOT PLATE and makes cups of instant coffee.

>ELVIS
>Damn! What it says here, is that you can bury some dude, and if he gets the right tanna leaves and spells said over him and such bullshit, he can come back to life thousands of years later. And to stay alive, he has to suck on the souls of the living, and that if the souls are small, his life force doesn't last long. Small. What's that mean?

>JACK
>Read on . . . No, never mind, I'll tell you.

Jack hands Elvis his CUP of coffee and sits down on the bed next to him.

>JACK (cont'd)
>Before I do, want a Ding-Dong?

Elvis looks at Jack suspiciously.

>JACK (cont'd)
>Not mine. The chocolate kind. Well, I guess mine is chocolate, now that I have been dyed.

>ELVIS
>You got Ding-Dongs?

>JACK
>Couple of Pay Days and a box of Baby Ruth's . . .

Jack shoots him a naughty smile.

>JACK (cont'd)
>Which will it be? Let's get decadent.

Elvis licks his lips.

                    ELVIS
          I'll take the Baby Ruth.

Jack reaches into his desk drawer, pulls out a shiny new BOX of "Baby Ruth" candy bars, and hands one to Elvis.

Elvis savors the candy, gumming it sloppily, sipping his coffee between bites.

Jack, coffee cup balanced on his knee, a Baby Ruth in one mitt, expounds...

                    JACK
          Small souls means those without much fire for life.
          You know a place like that?

                    ELVIS
          If souls were fires, they couldn't burn much lower
          than in here.

                    JACK
          Exactamundo. What we've got here in Shady Rest
          is an Egyptian soul sucker of some sort. A mummy
          hiding out, coming in here to feed on the sleeping.
          It's perfect, you see. The souls are little, and don't
          provide him with much. If this thing comes back
          two or three times in a row to wrap his lips around
          some elder's asshole, that elder is going to die pretty
          soon, and who's the wiser?

                                        SMASH CUT TO:

INTERIOR—KEMOSABE'S ROOM—NIGHT
Kemosabe, asleep in bed, is awakened by the scuttling sound and a swirling wind blowing around his room. As he reaches consciousness he notices something and looks over to see...

BUBBA HO-TEP bent over a figure (Kemosabe's roommate) in the darkness on the floor.

Suddenly, the Mummy senses Kemosabe and whirls around to look at him.

Kemosabe recoils at the rotted face of Bubba Ho-tep. He takes a deep breath and steadies himself, then... surreptitiously he slides his hands up to his headboard, where his twin Fanner .50's are slung in their holsters. The old man wraps his fingers around the hand grips and with amazing agility for a man of his age, suddenly...

Kemosabe whips both guns out of their holsters, spins them on his index fingers, and then clutches them....barrels trained dead-to-rights on the forehead of the Mummy.

                KEMOSABE
Asshole.

Kemosabe begins firing caps.

                                CUT BACK TO:

INT JACK'S ROOM—NIGHT
Jack is still talking to Elvis, but now, he's on a roll...

                JACK
Our mummy may not be getting much energy out of this, way he would with big souls, but the prey is easy. A mummy couldn't be too strong, really. Mostly just husk. But we're pretty much that way ourselves. We're not too far off from being living mummies.

                ELVIS
And with new people coming in all the time, he can keep this up forever, this soul robbing.

                JACK
That's right. Because that's what we're brought here for. To get us out of the way until we die. And the ones that don't die first of disease, or just plain old age, he gets.

This point rings true as Elvis and Jack sit and ponder it awhile.

> ELVIS
> That's why he doesn't bother the nurses and aides and administrators . . . he can conduct his business unsuspected.

> JACK
> That, and they're not asleep. He has to get you when you're sleeping or unconscious.

> ELVIS
> All right, but the thing throws me, Jack, is how does an ancient Egyptian end up in an East Texas rest home, and why is he writin' on shit house walls?

> JACK
> (shrugs)
> He went to take a crap, got bored, and wrote on the wall. Probably wrote on pyramid walls, centuries ago.

> ELVIS
> What would he crap? It's not like he'd eat?

> JACK
> He eats souls, so I assume, he craps soul residue. And what that means to me is, you die by his mouth, you don't go to the other side, or wherever souls go. He digests the souls till they don't exist anymore.

> ELVIS
> (ruminates)
> And you're just so much toilet water decoration.

> JACK
> Speaking of toilets . . .

Jack shuffles toward the bathroom. As he does, he continues to talk.

> JACK (cont'd)
> That's the way I've got it worked out. He's just like anyone else when he wants to take a dump. He likes a nice clean place with a flush. They didn't have that in his time.

Elvis finishes off the Baby Ruth and sips his coffee.

We can hear Jack urinating in the bathroom.

Suddenly, Elvis is pulled out of his considerations. From out in the hall...

THE NOISE begins again.

Elvis feels goosebumps travel up his spine. The hairs on the back of his neck and arms stand up. He leans forward and puts his hands on his walker and pulls himself upright.

Jack moves out from the bathroom and stops. He listens intently as the noise intensifies. Jack grabs hold of Elvis' shoulder protectively.

> JACK (cont'd)
> Don't go out in the hall.

> ELVIS
> I'm not asleep.

> JACK
> That doesn't mean it won't hurt you.

> ELVIS
> It my ass, there isn't any mummy from Egypt.

Elvis starts to move toward the open door as Jack grabs hold of a heavy wood CANE and presses himself back defensively into the corner alcove of his room.

JACK
(shrugs)
Nice knowing you, Elvis.

Elvis inches the walker forward. He is almost to the open door when he looks around the corner and...

INTERIOR—HALLWAY—NIGHT
At the end of the hallway, in a pool of darkness is A FIGURE in shadows.

CU ELVIS in the door frame, as he peers intently into the gloom.

Suddenly, the HALL LIGHTS go dim and start to sputter. With a LOUD CRACK, one of the FLUORESCENT LIGHT FIXTURES on the ceiling shorts out... SPARKS dance from it.

CU ELVIS—Slow motion

He looks up at the sparks as the light fixture begins to STROBE, blinking on and off.

Down at the end of the hallway, the THING begins to walk, stumble, and shuffle toward him. Its legs move like Elvis' own, meaning not too good, and yet, there is something about its locomotion that is impossible to identify. Stiff, but ghostly smooth.
The FIGURE is dressed in nasty looking JEANS, a black SHIRT, a black cowboy HAT that comes down so low it covers where the thing's eyebrows should be. It wears large cowboy BOOTS with the toes curled up.

As the THING comes even with the doorway...

Elvis finds that he can't move... can't scoot ahead another inch. He's rooted in his tracks.

The THING stops and cautiously turns its head on its apple stem neck and looks at Elvis with empty eye sockets, revealing that it is, in fact, uglier than Lyndon Johnson.

Suddenly, Elvis is surging forward as if on a zooming camera dolly, and . . .

Elvis is plunging into the thing's right eye socket, which swells speedily to the dimensions of a vast canyon bottomed by blackness.

CUT TO:

—MONTAGE SEQUENCE OF FAST CUTS
Down Elvis goes, spinning and spinning, and out of the emptiness rushes the resin-scented memories of Ho-tep—

Pyramids, stone temples, a sphynx—

The Pharoah's palace—

The young king Amen Ho-tep brooding on his throne—

Egyptian handmaidens catering to his every desire—

Ho-tep's own mummification—-only he is alive . . . as the shrouded priests tear his brain out through his nostril!—

A great silver BUS lashed hard by black rain—

A crumbling BRIDGE and a charge of dusky water and a gleam of silver.

Then there is DARKNESS, and then—

There comes a POPPING SOUND in rapid succession—

Elvis feels himself whirling even faster, spinning backwards out of that deep memory canyon of the dusty head, and . . .

END MONTAGE

INTERIOR—HALLWAY—NIGHT

Now, Elvis stands once again within the framework of his walker, and...

THE MUMMY—for Elvis no longer denies to himself that it is such—turns its head away and begins to move again, to shuffle, to flow, to stumble, to glide away down the hall. On the floor...

TWIN SCARAB BEETLES scurry along, chasing after their master.

A SOUND of a Pop! Pop! Pop! is heard. As the thing moves on...

Elvis compels himself to lift his walker and advance out into the hall.

Jack slips up beside him, and they see...

The Mummy, in cowboy clothes, traveling toward the exit door at the back of the home. When it comes to the locked door...

The Mummy leans against where the door meets the jam and twists and writhes, squeezing through the invisible crack where the two connect.

THE POPPING SOUND goes on, and...

Elvis turns his head in that direction, and there, in his MASK, his double studded HOLSTER belted around his waist, and pajamas, stands...

KEMOSABE, a silver "Fanner-Fifty" revolver in either hand. He is popping caps rapidly at where the Mummy has departed, the black-spotted red cap rolls flowing out from behind the hammers of his revolvers in smoky relay.

KEMOSABE
Asshole! Asshole!

And then, Kemosabe quivers, drops both hands, pops a cap from each gun toward the ground, stiffens, and collapses.

The HALL LIGHTS tremble back to normal illumination.
Time stands still as Jack and Elvis gape at Kemosabe's prone form.

Suddenly, the Administrator, two NURSES and two AIDES come running from the office out into the hall. They sprint toward the figure lying in the center of the hallway.

They roll Kemosabe over and drive their palms against his chest, but he doesn't breathe again. No more Hi-Yo-Silver.

> ELVIS
> (Voice Over)
> Kemosabe was dead of a ruptured heart before he hit the floor; gone down and out with both guns blazing, soul intact.

The nurses sigh over him and cluck their tongues, and finally one of them reaches over and lifts Kemosabe's mask, pulls it off his head and drops it on the floor, nonchalantly, and without respect—revealing his identity.

DISSOLVE TO:

INTERIOR—HALLWAY—LATER
Elvis and Jack are surrounded by aides and administrators, interrogating them. In SLOW MOTION the camera moves around the group and in on our heroes.

> ELVIS
> (Voice Over)
> Once again, we got scolded, but this time we got quizzed about what had happened to Kemosabe, but neither of us told the truth. Who was going to believe a couple of nuts? Elvis and Jack Kennedy explaining that Kemosabe was gunning for a mummy in cowboy duds, some kind of Bubba Ho-Tep? So, what we did, was lie.

CUT TO:
INTERIOR—HALLWAY—EVEN LATER STILL
Elvis, using his walker for support, gets down on his knee and picks up Kemosabe's discarded mask.

Elvis stares grimly at Kemosabe's mask which he clutches in his hands. Jack moves up alongside and puts a hand on Elvis' shoulder. As the two old men begin to shuffle off together down the dim hall, Elvis pockets the mask inside his robe.

FADE OUT:
EXTERIOR—REST HOME—DAY
The two Attendants exit the Mud Creek Shady Rest carrying Kemosabe's sheet-covered CORPSE on a stretcher.

>ATTENDANT #1
>You know, life sure is fleeting.

>ATTENDANT #2
>What?

>ATTENDANT #1
>Life. You know, one minute you're here . . .

Attendant #1 makes a grand gesture with one hand to emphasize his point.

>ATTENDANT #1 (cont'd)
>. . . and the next minute you're . . .

Suddenly he loses control of his end of the stretcher. The two Attendants accidentally bump into the porch railing, tip the stretcher and Kemosabe's sheet-covered corpse slides off into the bushes below.

>ATTENDANT #2
>Goddammit!!

The two men quickly dash down the stairs and awkwardly struggle to retrieve the corpse from the bushes. With difficulty, they manage to manhandle the body onto the stretcher. They drag the stretcher over to the hearse and roughly shove the corpse inside.

> ATTENDANT #2 (CONT'D)
> Christ you are one fuckin' idiot.

Attendant #2 slams the hearse door shut and they climb into the coach. As the hearse rumbles off,

Elvis, wearing a KHAKI BUSH JACKET over his pajamas, clumps outside with his walker. He scans the horizon and sniffs the air.

Elvis looks up at the sky.

POV—ELVIS—of the massive clouds.

Elvis reaches down and picks some flowers, and smells them.

The nurse comes outside and stops and stares at Elvis.

> NURSE
> Mr. Presley, you look so much stronger. But you shouldn't stay out too long. It's almost time for your nap, and for us to do that, you know . . .

In a sudden explosion of fury . . .

> ELVIS
> Fuck off, you patronizing bitch. I'm tired of your shit. I'll lube my own crankshaft from now on. You treat me like a baby again, I'll wrap this goddamn walker right around your head.

The nurse stands stunned, then turns and walks away quietly.

Elvis stares after her as she leaves and with a harummph, grabs hold of his walker and clumps away.

CUT TO:
EXTERIOR— BACK OF REST HOME—DAY
Thirty minutes later, Elvis reaches the back of the home and the door through which the Mummy had departed. He inspects the door, then grabs the door handle and shakes it.

The door is still locked, and . . .

Elvis stands looking at it in amazement. He sticks his finger in the quarter-inch crack between door and frame.

>   ELVIS
> How in hell did that mummy do that?

Elvis looks down at the concrete at the back of the door, then the surrounding bushes. No clues there. He turns and uses the walker to travel toward . . .

CUT TO:
EXTERIOR—FORESTED AREA—DAY
There stands a growth of TREES out back, a clump of pin-oaks and sweet gums and hickory nut trees that shoulder on either side of the large creek that flows behind the home.

The ground tips sharply here, and for a moment . . . Elvis hesitates, then reconsiders.

>   ELVIS
>   (mutters)
>   Well, what the hell . . .

Elvis plants the walker and starts going forward, the ground sloping ever more dramatically.

EXTERIOR—CREEKSIDE HILL—DAY
He starts to slide but, like a skier, he quickly learns how to jam the legs of the walker into the soft loam to slow and control his movement.

EXTERIOR—CREEK BANK—DAY

Elvis reaches the bank of the creek and comes to a gap in the trees. He is exhausted.

He turns and looks back up the path he came.

ELVIS—POV—of a very steep hill he will have to climb to get out of there.

Elvis looks over the bank of the creek. It is quite a drop here.

The CREEK itself is narrow, and on either side of it is a gravel-littered six-feet of shore. To his left, where the creek runs beneath a bridge, Elvis can see where a MASS OF WEEDS AND MUD have gathered over time, and he can see . . .

SOMETHING SHINY in their midst . . . some kind of vehicle bumper. Below that he can see a LICENSE PLATE.

Elvis eases to the ground inside his walker and sits there and looks at the water churning along.

A HUGE WOODPECKER laughs in a tree nearby and a jay yells at a smaller bird to leave his territory.

                        ELVIS
    (to himself)
    Where'd ole Bubba Ho-Tep go? Where'd he come
    from? How in hell did he get here?

The camera moves into a CU on Elvis' eyes as he recalls what he had seen inside the mummy's mind.

                              FLASHBACK TO:

MONTAGE OF FAST CUTS
  —The silver bus
  —The rain driving against the bus windshield,
  —The shattered bridge up ahead,

—The wash of water and mud.

BACK ON ELVIS at creek bank

>   ELVIS
> (to himself)
> Well, now wait a minute . . .

Elvis looks at essentially the same shots as he saw in the flashback, only daytime.

—The Water
—Mud
—And a bridge, though it's not broken
—And then the SHINY SOMETHING in the midst of all those leaves and limbs and collected debris.

Elvis stares hard at all these items, trying to make a connection. After a time, he takes a deep breath, turns and makes his way back up the hill.

CUT TO:

INTERIOR—ELVIS' ROOM—EVENING
Elvis is covered in sweat and his clothes are dirty as he clumps to his bed and flops down. He lets out a groan as he unfastens his pants and eases down his underwear. Elvis peers down at his groin.

>   ELVIS
>   (Voice Over)
> It's a cancer . . . and they're keepin' it from me
> because I'm old and to them it don't matter. They
> think age will kill me first, and they're probably
> right. Well, suck them. I know what it is, and if it
> isn't, it might as well be.

Elvis reaches onto his bedside table, takes the JAR OF SALVE and begins doctoring the pus-filled lesion. He puts the salve away, and pulls up his underwear and pants, and fastens his belt.

Elvis grabs his TV remote off the dresser and clicks it on while he waits for dinner. As Elvis runs the channels, he hits upon...

INSERT—TV

      TV ANNOUNCER
       (Voice Over)
  Station K-R-O-P is proud to present the 24 Hour Elvis Presley Movie Marathon!!

A TITLE CARD wheels onscreen to read:

      24 Hour
     Elvis Presley
     Movie Marathon

The title card fades as a thumping rock beat cuts in and we super a selection of STOCK FOOTAGE shots.

     TV ANNOUNCER (cont'd)
  It's 24 Hours of Elvis...in the roles he made famous!

Stock Footage: A group of 1950's era TEENAGERS sit around a beach campfire as we see Elvis' silhouette in the foreground strumming a guitar.

     TV ANNOUNCER (cont'd)
  Watch that two-fisted Hound Dog, out strum...

Stock Footage: Several COWBOYS knock each other around a Western barroom.

     TV ANNOUNCER (cont'd)
  ...out-fight, out-race...

Stock Footage: 1950's era vintage RACE CARS hurtle around a race track.

                    TV ANNOUNCER (cont'd)
              . . . and out-wit the bad guys . . .

Stock Footage: Girls in bikinis dancing

                    TV ANNOUNCER (cont'd)
              . . . and at the same time watch the King slay the
              girls . . .

BACK ON ELVIS IN ROOM

Elvis looks at the TV, startled as a thought strikes him hard.

                              ELVIS
              (mutters)
              Shitty pictures man, every single one.

                         ELVIS (cont'd)
                         (Voice Over)
              Here I was complaining about loss of pride and how
              life had treated me, and now I realize I'd never had
              any pride . . . and much of how life had treated me
              had been quite good, and the bulk of the bad had
              been my own damn fault. I wished now I'd fired
              Colonel Parker, about the time I got into the pic-
              tures. The old fart had been a shark and a fool, and
              I'd been an even bigger fool for following him. If only
              I'd treated Priscilla right, and could tell my daughter
              I love her. Always the questions. Never the answers.
              Always the hopes. Never the fulfillments . . .

Elvis clicks off the set and drops the remote on the dresser just as . . .

Jack comes into the room. Dressed nattily in suit and tie, he has a folder under his arm. He looks like he is ready for a briefing at the White House.

                    JACK
I had that woman who calls herself my niece come
get me. She took me downtown this morning to the
newspaper morgue. She's been helping me do some
research.

                    ELVIS
On what?

                    JACK
On our mummy.

                    ELVIS
You know something about him?

                    JACK
I know plenty.

Jack pulls a chair up next to the bed, and . . .

Elvis uses the bed's lift button to raise his back and head so he can see what is in Jack's folder.
Jack opens the folder, takes out some clippings, and lays them on the bed.

Elvis examines them as Jack talks.

                    JACK (cont'd)
One of the lesser mummies, on loan from the
Egyptian government, was being circulated across
the United States. You know, museums, that kind
of stuff.

                    ELVIS
Yeah, you mean like King Tut?

                    JACK
More like King Tut's brother. His mummy was

flown or carried by train from state to state. When it got to Texas, it was stolen.

                    ELVIS
Stolen??

Elvis listens intently as Jack tells the tale.

                    JACK
Evidence points to it being stolen at night by a couple of guys in a silver bus.

                    ELVIS
The bus. I saw that . . . way back in the creek.

                    JACK
There was a witness. Some guy walking his dog or something. Anyway, the thieves broke in the museum and stole it, hoping to get a ransom. But in came the worst storm in East Texas history. You may remember it. Tornadoes. Rain. Hail.

Elvis shakes his head negatively.

                    JACK (cont'd)
No matter. It was one hell of a flood.

Elvis is thinking hard now . . .

                    ELVIS
Let me guess. The bus got washed away. I think I saw it today. Right out back in the creek. It must have washed up there years ago.

                    JACK
That confirms it. The bus was carried downstream. It lodged somewhere nearby, and the mummy was imprisoned by the debris.

ELVIS
It must have worked its way loose. But how did it come alive? And how did I end up inside its memories?

JACK
The speculation is broader here, but from what I've read, sometimes mummies were buried without their names, a curse put on their sarcophagus.

ELVIS
I bet our boy was one of them. While he was in the coffin, he was a drying corpse. But when the bus was washed off the road, the coffin was overturned, or broken open, and he was freed of coffin and curse.

JACK
He's free of his imprisonment, but he still needs souls.

ELVIS
And now, he's free to have them, and he'll keep on feeding unless he's finally destroyed . . .

JACK
You know, I think there's a part of him, oddly enough, that wants to fit in. To be human again. He doesn't entirely know what he's become.

ELVIS
That's why he's wearing them old cowboy clothes, probably copying the dress of one of his victims. So, what do we do Jack?

JACK
Changing rest homes might be a good idea. Can't think of much else. I will say this: Our mummy is a nighttime kind of guy.

Jack turns and starts to move toward the door.

                    JACK (cont'd)
          ... I'm going to sleep now. Set my alarm for before
          dark so I can fix myself a couple cups of coffee.

                         ELVIS
          Damn straight. He comes in tonight, I don't want
          him slapping his lips over my asshole.

                         JACK
          Yes... consider it. He's got the proverbial bird's
          nest on the ground here.

Elvis says nothing as they exchange grim looks. Jack turns and leaves.
Elvis nestles his head into the pillows and ruminates.

                         ELVIS
                      (Voice Over)
          What do I have left in life but this place? It ain't
          much of a home, but it's all I've got.

As Elvis gazes around his room, surveying his home, an anger builds
in him. He sits up and grabs hold of his walker. He raises himself
from the bed and starts across the room

                    ELVIS (cont'd)
          (growls)
          Well Goddammit! I'll be damned if I let a foreign,
          graffiti-writin', soul-suckin' sonofabitch in an
          oversized hat and boots take away my friend's souls
          and shit 'em down the visitors toilet!

Elvis stops at the bureau and looks at his telephone. The camera begins a slow move into his face and as a steely resolve crosses it...

                    ELVIS (cont'd)
                      (Voice Over)
          In the movies I always played heroic types. But
          when the stage lights went out, it was time for drugs

and stupidity and the coveting of women. Now it's time, time to be a little of what I'd always fantasized being:

A hero.

Elvis leans over, gets hold of his telephone and dials.

> JACK
> (Voice Over)

Hello.

> ELVIS

Mr. Kennedy. Ask not what your rest home can do for you. Ask what you can do for your rest home.

> JACK

Hey, you're copping my best lines.

> ELVIS

Well then, to paraphrase one of my own, "Let's take care of business."

> JACK

Just what are you gettin' at, Elvis?

> ELVIS

You know what I'm getting at, Mr. President.

Elvis draws a long, deep breath.

> ELVIS (cont'd)

We're gonna kill us a mummy.

CUT TO:

INTERIOR—JACK'S ROOM—NIGHT
Jack squints through his glasses and examines a piece of paper.

                    JACK
          Two bottles of rubbing alcohol?

                    ELVIS
          Check. And we won't have to toss it. Look here.

Elvis stands beside him. He reaches down to the floor and holds up a metal, pump, PAINT SPRAYER.

                    ELVIS (cont'd)
          Found this in the storage room.

                    JACK
          I thought they kept it locked.

                    ELVIS
          They do. But I stole a hair pin and picked the lock.

                    JACK
          Great! Matches?

                    ELVIS
          Check. I also scrounged a cigarette lighter.

                    JACK
          Good. Uniforms?

Elvis holds up a white, gabardine JUMPSUIT. The sequins and gold studs still glitter. He lays the jumpsuit on the bed.

                    ELVIS
          Big check on that, baby.

Jack holds up a dark grey business suit on a hanger, and then lays it beside the jumpsuit.

                    JACK
          I've got some nice shoes and a tie to go with it.

                    ELVIS
Check.

                    JACK
Scissors?

                    ELVIS
Check.

Jack looks over at this motorized WHEELCHAIR in the corner.

                    JACK
I've got my chair oiled and ready to roll.

Elvis spots the chair.

                    ELVIS
Good. We could use some wheels.

                    JACK
And I've looked up a few words of power in one of my magic books. I don't know if they'll stop a mummy, but they're supposed to ward off evil. I wrote them down, one for each of us.

Jack hands Elvis a folded PIECE OF PAPER.

                    ELVIS
We use what we got. Well then. Two forty-five A.M. out back?

                    JACK
Considering our rate of travel, we better start moving about two-thirty.

Elvis hesitates and looks Jack right in the eye.

ELVIS
Jack, do we know what the hell we're doing?

JACK
No, but they say fire cleanses evil. Let's hope "they", whoever they are, is right.

ELVIS
Check on that too. Synchronize watches.

Jack and Elvis synchronize their watches, and then Elvis moves toward the door.

ELVIS (cont'd)
Remember. The key words for tonight are "Caution" and "Flammable".

JACK
And also, "Watch Your Ass".

Elvis nods his head in agreement and clumps out the door.

FADE TO:

MOONRISE
A full moon rises over the East Texas pines.

CUT TO:

INSERT—CU on the rubber tip of a walker as it drops onto the polished black and white tile floor.

INSERT—CU on a wheelchair tire as it rolls into frame.

INTERIOR—HALLWAY—NIGHT
We see down the length of the dark, moonlit, empty hallway of the rest home.

Jack rolls around the corner in his motorized wheelchair. He looks presidential in his charcoal suit. The suit fits him well. He looks like a former president.

JFK (Ossie Davis) watches for the evil Egyptian, Bubba Ho-Tep.

Walker in hand, Elvis rounds the corner. The gold studs of his jumpsuit dance in the dim light. He's got the studded cape around his shoulders and, even with the walker, he's got a bit of a strut. Elvis is wearing his gold-framed GLASSES and his white jumpsuit with scarf, belt and zippered white boots. Elvis' suit is open at the front and hangs loose on him, except at the belly. Around his neck hangs a leather MEDICINE BAG of sorts, which is stuffed inside his jumpsuit and sticks out.

The two friends move stoically toward camera with a sense of purpose. Music builds as our warriors head into battle to face a showdown with the dark unknown.

CUT TO:

INTERIOR—REST HOME side DOOR AREA—NIGHT
Jack wedges open the door to the ALARM BOX. He reaches inside and flips a control switch. He nods to Elvis.

Using the scissors, Elvis gingerly cuts the alarm wires on the front door monitor. Once the wires are cut, Elvis pushes the compression lever on the door handle, and holds the door open as Jack drives his chair through.

CUT TO:

EXTERIOR—REST HOME SIDE PORCH AREA—NIGHT
Elvis empties the alcohol bottles into the reservoir of the paint sprayer.

Jack watches patiently from his wheelchair until Elvis' medicine bag catches his attention.

       JACK
 What's that thing hanging around your neck?

Elvis grabs the small leather pouch and holds it up for Jack to see.

       ELVIS
 Medicine bag. Injuns goin' into battle carry

'em. Filled with all kinds of lucky stuff, you know... mucho mojo...

Elvis reaches into the back and pulls out a few items. He opens his hand to reveal... Kemosabe's Lone Ranger Mask... and then, Bull's Purple Heart medal.

From the bottom of the medicine bag, Elvis pulls out a crumpled PHOTO and holds it up for Jack to see.

> ELVIS (cont'd)
> My daughter.

> JACK
> Yeah. I know. We weren't there for our kids when they needed us, were we?

Elvis nods, a look of sadness crossing his face.

> ELVIS
> If I could just talk to her again... tell her I love her... make things right somehow...

> JACK
> (nodding in sympathy)
> No time for regrets, Elvis. We were the best fathers we could be... under the circumstances...

Elvis places the photo back in the medicine bag and tucks it back into his jumpsuit.

> ELVIS
> Yeah, no time for regrets. We got business to take care of.

Elvis bends down on one knee and unscrews the lid of a large red GASOLINE CAN. He pours the flammable liquid into the paint sprayer tank.

                    ELVIS (cont'd)
          I stole it when the gardener wasn't looking.

Jack whistles as Elvis tops off the sprayer tank with the gasoline.

                         JACK
          It's gonna be one helluva barbecue.

Elvis twists shut the pneumatic lid of the paint sprayer. A shoulder strap made of a strip of torn sheet has been added to the device.

Elvis slings his weapon over his shoulder and reaches inside his belt. He pulls out a flattened, half-smoked STOGIE, which he'd been saving for a special occasion.

Elvis clenches the cigar between his teeth and looks at Jack.

                         ELVIS
          Let's do it, amigo.

Jack kicks the foot stanchions into place and rests his feet on them. He flips the "on" switch and twists the throttle. The wheelchair does an efficient 180 and Jack heads away from Elvis down the cement path.

                    ELVIS (cont'd)
          Hey Jack, I just got one last question . . . Marilyn?

Jack stops the wheelchair and looks back at Elvis quizzically.

                    ELVIS (cont'd)
          Marilyn Monroe . . . what was she like in the sack??

                         JACK
             (straight-faced)
          That is classified information . . . top secret.

Jack leans back slightly and flicks a switch on the arm rest.

                    JACK (cont'd)
         ... but between you and me ... Wow!!

A flicker of envy crosses Elvis' face.

The electric motor hums, and Jack drives off into the darkness.

                         ELVIS
              Hey Jack, watch your back.

As Jack disappears, Elvis checks his watch. He lets out a sigh.

                    ELVIS (cont'd)
              Gotta hump it.

Elvis clenches both hands on the walker and starts trucking.

                                                  CUT TO:
EXTERIOR—GROVES—NIGHT
Jack drives among the trees on the edge of the rest home. He peers into the darkness.

                                                  CUT TO:
EXTERIOR—BACK GATE—NIGHT
Out back, fifteen exhaustive minutes later, Elvis staggers up and settles in against the wooden gate. The shadows fall over him like an umbrella.

Elvis props the paint gun across the walker and uses his scarf to wipe the sheeting sweat off his forehead. He pulls out his matches, lights up his stogie and takes a puff.

POV—ELVIS

In the center of the grove of trees, seated in the wheelchair, very patient and still, is Jack. The moonlight spreads over Jack and makes him look like a concrete yard gnome.

An evil Egyptian entity, by the name of Bubba Ho-Tep (Bob Ivy), prowls the corridors of the rest home in search of his nemesis, a seventy-year-old Elvis Presley.

Elvis furrows his brow in anxiety and shakes his head.

>   ELVIS
>   (Voice Over)
> Shit . . . Bubba Ho-Tep comes out of that creek bed,
> he's gonna come out hungry and pissed, and when
> I try to stop him, he's gonna jam this paint can up
> my ass, then jam me and that wheelchair up Jack's
> ass.

Elvis puffs his cigar so fast it makes him dizzy. He looks back out at the creek bank, where the trees gape wide, and suddenly . . .

EXTERIOR—GROVES—NIGHT
Bubba Ho-tep appears out of the darkness, tottering up the hill from the creek bed. As the Mummy moves into the vicinity of an outdoor, gooseneck PATH LIGHT, the light begins to sputter and strobe.

As Elvis spots Bubba Ho-tep, his knees begin to clack together like stalks of ribbon cane rattling in a high wind.

The Mummy looks back at Elvis and then takes a step toward him.

Back on Elvis—The cigar falls from his lips.

Elvis nervously grabs the paint gun. He begins furiously pumping it. He jacks the paint injector lever and then rams open the paint valve. His weapon locked and loaded, he pushes the butt of it into his hip. He looks back up to see . . .

The Mummy is gone.

Elvis squints and then scans the grove, searching for a sign of the Mummy.

Nothing.

>   ELVIS
>   (muttered)

Shit.
(cries out)
Jack!!

CU JACK—Across the groves, Jack has nodded off and is snoring, slumped in his chair. Elvis' cry does not rouse Jack, who continues to doze.

Dismayed, Elvis takes a deep breath and clumps tentatively forward with his walker, moving in Jack's direction.

He crosses to a stand of trees and then suddenly . . .

Bubba Ho-tep looms up from the tree behind Elvis.

Elvis stops in his tracks sensing something is wrong.

A low growl escapes from the Mummy and as the creature reaches for Elvis . . .

Elvis whips up his walker, spins around and throws all his weight forward. He shoves the flimsy aluminum walker into the Mummy's neck and manages to pin the squirming Mummy up against the tree trunk.

Bubba Ho-tep leans forward, his jaws snapping, his teeth just inches from Elvis' face.

To Elvis' dismay, he realizes he has a tiger by the tail. There is no way he can out-muscle the writhing creature. Suddenly Elvis' strength gives out and Elvis is tossed backwards and lands on the ground in a heap.

ON JACK—Across the way, the sound of the commotion rouses Jack from his slumber . . . he looks over and . . .

POV JACK—He sees Elvis on the ground and the Mummy standing menacingly nearby.

BACK TO ELVIS—Gasping for breath, Elvis grabs hold of a nearby

Elvis (Bruce Campbell) prepares to battle against the evil Bubba Ho-Tep.

tree and manages to pull himself to his feet. Elvis looks around and sees that flight is not an option.

Elvis takes a deep breath, his face hardens.

>   ELVIS (cont'd)
> Don't make me use my stuff, baby.

Elvis slices the air with a few of his patented "stage karate chops". They actually look pretty decent. He tries a karate kick, but with a crack, his bum hip gives out.

The Mummy just stares at Elvis.

POV Elvis—The Mummy in foreground and then silently, about 30 yards behind him, Jack motors into view and stops.

The Mummy senses Jack, turns, looks and sees that he's being outflanked. The Mummy looks back at Elvis . . . thinks better of it, turns and moves toward Jack.

The Mummy passes behind a tree and . . . does not appear on the other side. The Mummy has vanished once more.

Jack scans the area but sees nothing.

>   JACK
> Where'd he go?

Elvis scans the area.

POV—Elvis—Bubba Ho-tep is nowhere to be seen.

>   JACK (cont'd)
>   (to Elvis)
> You stay put! I'll flush him out.

Jack decides to take action and jams down the throttle on his wheelchair and heads toward the point where Bubba Ho-tep disappeared.

As Elvis scans the area, he suddenly notices the Mummy lurking behind another tree.

> ELVIS
> (gasps)
> No, Jack...

Bubba Ho-tep sticks out his arm and clotheslines Jack Kennedy as he drives by.

Over goes the chair, and out flies Jack, crashing to the ground with a terrible, sickening thud.

Elvis recoils at this sight.

The wheelchair, minus its rider, tumbles over and comes upright. The throttle stuck open, the chair veers away.

Elvis watches in dawning horror that their plan has failed.

Bubba Ho-tep stalks toward the unconscious Jack.

Elvis frantically looks around himself for any kind of weapon he can use, when he notices the wheelchair... motoring his way!

He quickly turns himself into position and as the wheelchair drives up, he plops down into the seat. He reaches down and grabs hold of the paint sprayer and quickly slings it over his shoulder.

Elvis grabs the wheelchair JOYSTICK and throws the chair into a hard 180 turn and jams down on the throttle.

Back on Jack—

CU BUBBA HO-TEP moving in on Jack. As the Mummy comes down on him its mouth goes wide, then wider yet, and becomes...

A BLACK TOOTHLESS VACUUM.

Elvis in the wheelchair races toward Jack.

Bubba Ho-tep's mouth goes down over Jack's face, and as Bubba Ho-Tep begins to suck . . .

Elvis skids the wheelchair to a stop, directly in front of the Mummy. Elvis whistles and Bubba Ho-tep looks up from his business with Jack.

The camera moves into a CU of Elvis' steely expression.

                      ELVIS (cont'd)
Come and get it, you un-dead sack of shit.

Bubba Ho-tep staggers to his feet and screams something at Elvis in Egyptian. As the Mummy shrieks . . .

Elvis sees the words literally jump out of Bubba Ho-Tep's mouth. VISIBLE HIEROGLYPHICS, like dark beetles and sticks, materialize in the air beside Bubba Ho-tep's mouth, and then disintegrate as the sound fades.

SUPER SUBTITLE:
      "By the unwinking red eye of Ra!"

Bubba Ho-tep moves for Elvis.

Elvis waits until the last moment and then quickly jerks up the business end of the paint gun and squeezes the trigger.

The gasoline-alcohol mixture squirts from the sprayer and . . . strikes Bubba Ho-tep directly in the face.

The Mummy recoils from the noxious liquid dripping from his face.

Suddenly Elvis whips the chrome lighter up from his lap, flips open the lid and ignites it.

                        ELVIS (cont'd)
         Sorry, man.

Elvis hurls the lighter and as it strikes him, the Mummy's head bursts into a brilliant inferno of flame.

Screaming in agony, Bubba Ho-tep turns to flee, but just manages to fan the flames as he runs. The Mummy throws himself to the ground and manages to stop the burning.

Elvis lets out a deep breath and turns his attention to his fallen comrade.

Elvis wheels over to Jack and pulls to a stop beside him. Jack is on the ground and Elvis observes the awful shape he is in. Elvis swallows hard, then leans forward and whispers . . .

                        ELVIS (cont'd)
         (whispers)
         Mr. Kennedy.
Jack's eyelids flutter. He can barely move his head, and something grates in his neck when he does. His eyes look up to Elvis.

                        JACK
         (raspy whisper)
         The President is soon dead.

Jack's clenched fist opens, and he passes a wad of paper to Elvis.

                        JACK (cont'd)
         Now it's up to you, Elvis. You got to get him. You
         got to take care . . . of . . . business . . .

Jack's body goes loose, his head rolls back and his eyes close.

Elvis swallows hard again, slowly raises his hand and salutes Jack.

> ELVIS
> Mr. President.

Elvis leans forward and picks up the paper Jack dropped. He gets to his feet and looking over at the smoldering Mummy on the ground, Elvis reads it aloud to himself in the moonlight . . .

> ELVIS (cont'd)
> (reading)
> You nasty thing from beyond the dead,
> No matter what you think or do,
> Good things will never come to you.

Elvis skeptically ponders this and then continues reading.

> ELVIS (cont'd)
> And if evil is your black design,
> You can bet,
> The goodness of the Light Ones,
> Will kick your bad behind.

Elvis curses under his breath.

> ELVIS (cont'd)
> That's it? That's the chant against evil from the Book of Souls? Yeah, right, boss. And what kind of decoder ring does that one come with? Shit, it doesn't even rhyme well.

Elvis senses something and looks up to see . . .

Bubba Ho-tep's flames have gone out. The Mummy staggers to his feet. His head is hissing grey smoke. He turns to face Elvis. Bubba Ho-tep's face now looks like charred beef jerky.

Standing defiantly, the mummy raises an arm and shakes a fist. He yells, and once again . . . the hieroglyphics leap out of his mouth. The animated characters dance in a row, briefly—

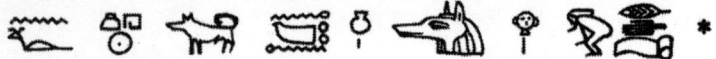

SUPERIMPOSE SUBTITLE:
"Eat the dog dick of Anubis, you ass wipe!"

The hieroglyphics vanish.

A grim expression settles in on Elvis' face as he stares down the mummy. Elvis crumples and tosses away the paper with the magic words on it.

                    ELVIS (cont'd)
  (Mutters)
  This is dog shit.

Elvis drops into the seat of the wheelchair and takes a deep breath.

                    ELVIS (cont'd)
  What's needed here is A-C-T-I-O-N.

Elvis jams down the lever and gives the wheelchair full throttle.

The wheelchair burns rubber, the tires catch and as the vehicle accelerates, the small front tires lift off the ground. Doing a "wheelie", Elvis' thunders forward, his white scarf fluttering in the wind.

Elvis lets loose a shriek . . . a Rebel Yell.

Bubba Ho-tep sees . . .

Elvis coming on strong, chair geared to the max, hefting the paint sprayer, gripped tightly in one hand. As he is about to hit the defiant Mummy . . .

Bubba Ho-tep leaps into the air and lands on top of the wheelchair.

As the wheelchair screams through the night, Elvis finds himself face-to-face with the angry Egyptian, Bubba Ho-tep. With one of his skeletal claws, the Mummy grabs Elvis by the neck.

POV—the wheelchair is headed straight for the edge of the cliff.

With his right hand unwaveringly jamming down on the throttle, Elvis jerks up his left hand and fires the paint sprayer right into Bubba Ho-tep's face.

The Mummy knocks the sprayer out of his hand.

Elvis responds with a savage karate chop to the thing's face.

The Mummy claws at him but Elvis manages to unload a looping right hook to the side of the Mummy's head.

EXTERIOR—CREEKSIDE HILL—NIGHT
Without slowing down a bit, at full speed, the wheelchair hits the lip of the hill bank in a flash of moonlight.

Bubba Ho-tep, Elvis and the chair are propelled through the air. They hit the steep hillside and tumble down.

Elvis screams as the hard ground and sharp stones, branches and sticks batter his body like a pinata.

Like a snowball, Elvis, Mummy and wheelchair tumble down the steep hillside.

EXTERIOR—CREEK BANK—NIGHT
The wheelchair rolls into the creek.

Elvis stops sliding and finds himself immobilized, close to the creek with Bubba Ho-tep slumped nearby.

Elvis gasps for breath and feels a sharp, stinging pain in his side. He looks down and is stunned to find one of his RIBS, broken and protruding from the side of his chest.

The Mummy comes to life, turns, and begins crawling toward him. His eyes pierce Elvis with a penetrating stare.

Elvis grabs hold of the paint gun and blasts Bubba Ho-tep once more in the face with another blast of the flammable mixture.

The Mummy grabs Elvis by the neck.

Bubba Ho-tep grabs hold of a HUNK OF WOOD that has washed up on the edge of the creek. Its arm comes around and . . . hits Elvis on the side of the head with the wood.

Elvis falls backward and the paint sprayer flies from his hands.

As Bubba Ho-tep leans over him Elvis desperately clutches for the paint sprayer. It is just out of reach. As Elvis stretches, his fingers touch the pump handle and grab hold of it . . . but the paint can tips over and the flammable liquids spill onto the creek bank and flow downhill.

The Mummy winds up and whacks Elvis again across the forehead with the hunk of wood.

Elvis' eyes flutter and roll up into his head. Everything begins to spin as Elvis starts to lose consciousness. The fire-singed Bubba Ho-tep just looks at his prey, dispassionately.

>   ELVIS
>   (Voice Over)
> I felt myself goin' out. But I knew if I did, not only was I a dead sonofabitch, but so was my soul. I'd be just so much crap; . . . no after-life, no reincarnation, no angels with harps. Whatever lay beyond would not be known to me. It would all end right here for Elvis Aron Presley. Nothing left but a quick flush.

A grim determination appears on Elvis' face and with sudden vigor, his left hand shoots up and grabs the Mummy by the neck.

                    ELVIS (cont'd)
  T.C.B, baby.

Elvis uncorks a sharp left cross which tags the Mummy right on the chin. The Mummy tumbles backward.

Elvis quickly reaches inside his open jumpsuit and grasps the folder of matches.

Bubba Ho-tep scrambles to his feet and looms over Elvis, eyes blazing with hate.

The match ignites and Elvis holds it up for the Mummy to see.

                    ELVIS (cont'd)
        Your soul suckin' days are over, amigo.

Elvis touches the burning match to the pool of spilled gasoline. The pool ignites and a burst of flame races downhill to the Mummy's feet. The gasoline on Bubba Ho-tep's body calls the flames to it, and suddenly . . .

Bubba Ho-tep bursts into a stalk of flame. With a shriek the Mummy is immolated and staggers toward the creek.

Elvis recoils from the burning blast of heat.

As Bubba Ho-tep burns, Elvis can hear the screams of the undead surround him as the souls of the Mummy's victims are released.

The fiery inferno that was Bubba Ho-tep topples forward and plunges into the creek in a blast of hot steam.

The wailing fades as Elvis becomes aware that Bubba Ho-Tep is gone. He leans up and sees the charred and still simmering remnants of

Bubba Ho-tep floating on the water.

Elvis struggles to get himself up on one elbow and looks down at . . . Bubba Ho-tep's corpse, dissolving more rapidly as the current is carrying it away.

Elvis falls over on his back. He takes another look at the BLOODY WOUND in his chest where a rib is broken out through the skin.

> ELVIS (cont'd)
> (Voice Over)
> I felt something inside gratin' against something soft. I felt like a water balloon with a hole poked in it. I was going down for the last count, and I knew it.

Elvis lets his head drop back onto the ground.

> ELVIS (cont'd)
(a bit delirious)
But I've still got my soul. Still mine. All mine. And the folks up there at Shady Rest, they have theirs too, and they'll keep 'em . . . every single one.

Elvis stares up at the stars between the forked and twisted boughs of an oak. He can see a lot of those beautiful stars, and . . .

POV—OF THE NIGHT SKY

The constellations shimmer and then, strangely, begin to move. The stars swirl into a glimmering pattern of hieroglyphics . . . Egyptian hieroglyphics!

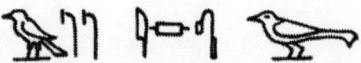

Elvis stares hard at the hieroglyphics, pondering them.

Elvis smiles.

POV—OF THE NIGHT SKY

A subtitle is superimposed over the starry hieroglyphics.

ALL IS WELL.

He stares into the bright starlight and as the meaning of the hieroglyphics sinks in, Elvis utters . . .

>ELVIS
>Thank you. Thank you very mu . . .

Elvis closes his eyes.

CUT TO CREDITS:

ROLL END CREDITS CRAWL

FADE OUT.

FADE IN FINAL CARD:

Elvis returns in:
BUBBA NOSFERATU
"CURSE OF THE SHE-VAMPIRES"
Starring Sebastian Haff

THE END